Dedication Page
This book is dedicated
To all Fans
Of the King of Pop
Michael J. Jackson

Additional Writing credits by Carol Denise Mitchell

Mitchell is an honored member of the African American Literature Book Club, (aalbc) http://authors.aalbc.com/carol.htm, September, 2006 News Letter named Mitchell, one of their "Authors You Should Know," for her comprehensive handbook, "Your Rights," regarding Employee employment rights.

Additional Writing Credits:

AC Associated Content, The People's Media Company (Internet) "Dream Office, the Reality of a Dream," April 5, (2007)
Helium Publication, (Internet) Resource based knowledge "Dealing With Wrongful Termination of Employment," January 01, (2007)
What Happened to Suzy, Carlton Press, (1995).
Mitchell resides in Concord, California near the San Francisco Bay Area, where she is at work on a wide range of fascinating writing projects

CAROL DENISE MITCHELL

THE LOVE HE SAVED

CAROL MITCHELL BOOKS

An Imprint of ©CDM3Publishers

This book is a work of fiction. The characters, incidents, and dialogue are artistic, written creations and are not to be construed as real. Any resemblance to actual events or persons, living or dead, is entirely coincidental.

CARROL MITCHELL BOOKS
An Imprint of CDM3Publishers
Post Office Box 484
Concord, California 94521-0484

ISBN 0-9786258-3-8
ISBN-13 978-0-9786258-3-2

Printed in the United States of America

Visit Carol Denise Mitchell on the World Wide Web at www.acceptedltr.com

10 9 8 7 6 5 4 3 2 1

EARLY PRAISE FOR CAROL DENISE MITCHELL's

THE LOVE HE SAVED

"Just when you thought you have read everything about Michael Jackson…Along comes Frankie Mae…She is a refreshing and most welcomed find…Readers will fall in love with Michael Jackson all over again!"

Gary G. Tavares
CEO & Founder of Tavares Entertainment, LLC
www.tavaresentertainment.net

BY

Carol Denise Mitchell

What Happened to Suzy

Your Rights, What Employers Do Not Want You to Know

Rovella Starr, (A Love-Starved Bitch)

A Love Worth Fighting For

ATTENTION: ORGANIZATIONS AND CORPORATIONS

Most Carol Mitchell Books are available at special quantity discounts for bulk purchases for sales promotions, premiums, or fund-raising. For information, please call or write

Special Markets Department, CDM3Publishers,
Post Office Box 484, Concord, California 94521
Telephone: 925-435-8699

Foreword

"I love my father. I don't know him the way I'd like to," Michael Jackson told Oprah Winfrey in an interview that took place on February 10, 1993. This is not what the media wants to hear!

Michael Jackson maintained his enormous fame amidst constant scrutiny and unending questions about his personal life. From Joseph to the women he loved to his skin color, the public could not get enough. He was a man who told Oprah he adored family life but was married to his work. For a man who admitted becoming the emotion of his sound – I was most impressed with the sides of Michael Jackson that none of us knew about, i.e., his secret loves. I was pleased to learn that he celebrated his race and was most fond of having ***"Learned how to Moonwalk from black kids in the ghetto."***

For a man who never got the chance to be a kid he observed children envying not having the playful formative years that mean so much to those who had childhoods. The media seized upon Michael's fascination with youth and with fantasy occasionally interpreting his truths into behavior that Michael Jackson was proven innocent of. As an adolescent who was too famous to live a normal life, Michael Jackson told Oprah that it was the public that wanted to keep him young forever. Concerning his love life, he said he dated ***Brooke Shields*** in 1993 and ***another girl.*** According to her own revelation, ***Frankie Mae*** could have been the "other girl," that Michael Jackson referenced in this world renowned interview. Read the book and then you decide if Frankie Mae was the love of Michael Jackson's life. Enjoy!

For Michael Joseph Jackson

"Legendary King of Pop"

1958-2009

Rest in Peace

RIP

OPENING

The Love He Saved

How did I know that the guy in the expensive limo who was checking me out was Michael Jackson? Let me say this: Nobody could miss the famous studded silver glove that panned against that car's tinted window. Besides, I had been waiting for this moment for so long, the shock value would not be there when it happened. The man in the expensive ride who was trailing me on the Santa Monica freeway was Michael Jackson, and everybody knew that I had been waiting for this my whole life. No sense pretending or setting this up like I was star-struck or something. I wasn't hoping for anything. Since 1972 as a seventeen-year-old, I had had plans of being with Michael Jackson. By the time the opportunity became a real-life event, I was ready. Granted, I may not have had my hair or outfit right, but I was ready!

I would have left anyone for him just like anybody else with good sense would have if that special moment had transpired. I had rehearsed everything I'd do if I ever met him for real, for Michael Jackson was the man for me no matter what.

Sorry – my Michael Jackson song, "Dancing Machine," is on KBLX and I have to get up and do a little popping and snapping. I'll be right back to finish the book. Hold on . . .

Ten minutes later . . .

I'm back. Sorry for the break, but that was my man. I am older now and I can't bust out the moves like I used to, but I tried. It has only been three months since his death, and as you can see, I have not gotten over it yet. Anyway, black or white, I was about to hook up with Michael Jackson! And you will not believe how it all happened.

~~~

On the eventful day that changed our lives in the '80s, my destiny was sealed because this was the day *he* had been waiting for. Somehow Michael Jackson already knew me, and in opposition to my own fantastic dream, the superstar was a fan of mine. As unbelievable as this may seem, from what he told me on that fateful meeting day, I was his picture-perfect average girl with the torn-up look who was perfect enough to keep our relationship the mystery that it needed to be. He followed me on the freeway for miles, flirting with me like we were making a video or something. Seeing him was an incredible dream for a girl that average guys passed
~~~

over at school and talked about like a dog.

"Look at Frankie Mae – her hair is so short she looks sick," Darnell chimed in one day.

"You think that's bad, look at those jacked-up teeth. Who would ever want that?" Cornell asked Darnell.

All of my prom dreams were decided and squashed in eleventh grade. I was so forgettable in high school that guys would have paid this ugly girl not to ask them out. At age seventeen I had no problem checking out of school. On the same day I dropped out, I was about to be beaten up because I didn't know at the time who sang a song called "One Bad Apple." Well, of course the fight going down was about Michael Jackson. Some of us thought it was Michael on the spin, and others (like me), thought it was not.

That aside, I loved Michael Jackson before he knew I existed. From a fan perspective, my dreams of loving him in real life were far-fetched ones that millions of fans entertained. However, I had imagined everything I'd do and say to him if I met him live. In high school, each team I knew had a dream about meeting the Jacksons. It was not cool to not know all the brothers or all of their hit songs. We had been star-struck since I was sixteen years old. Whereas loving Michael Jackson was puppy love for most teens, to me it was love for the ages. Each poster or magazine I ran home from school with meant more than anything to me. Something mystical and magical entered my mind.

I actually dreamed I'd meet Michael Jackson and that we'd soon fall in love. No other love flowed as deeply as our love did; our connection was instant from the start of our eventual meeting. Dreams and fan idolization would indeed materialize out of pure, undiluted, love-starved Synergy.

I know it's going to be hard for people to believe we had an affair that lasted almost twenty years without anyone finding out about it. For all intents and purposes, as much as I wanted to be prepared when I met Michael Jackson, as a teen I did not have my shit together, and ladies, it did not matter, for the meeting would take place when cheerleaders were young mothers and Cornell and Darnell would be cut from two minor training camp football teams. My family moved to southern California from Gary, Indiana, in the '60s with a teen who hated them for leaving the town of the Jacksons. Even small-time Jacksons were bigger than most huge stars are today. Quiet as it is kept, the town knew long before the chart-topping hits that the Jackson Clan was a special group of talented kids who were about to get things really jumping. The way they practiced in that small house that Jermaine told *Larry King* was the size of a two-car garage, no doubt this secluded family was headed straight for greatness and the lawns of Hollywood.

We left before the Jacksons did for Watts, California. This smart move by my parents did not go over well until my mother and father moved our family of three to Pomona, California, three days after a 72-hour riot almost consumed Watts. My two older brothers,

Tim and Walter, were twins and finished high school at Compton High in 1966, the year we left Los Angeles. Using all-expenses-paid scholarships from the United Negro College Fund (UNCF), they both graduated from college and later became successful Atlanta attorneys.

Left to fend for myself, I cried like a baby when my mother dropped Tim and Walter off at the Oakland Airport where they'd be headed for Atlanta. Both brothers had supported my love for Michael Jackson. Each of them bought me teen magazines and would help me pin posters to my blue bedroom walls. Without my brothers' unending protection and support, I lacked the self-esteem to have or put in motion a serious life plan after fantasizing over Michael Jackson.

Two years after my brothers' departure, I married early and died young in spirit. My father left my mother for a fifteen-year-old teen I had gone to junior high school with. The separation killed my brothers; the issue caused my family to drift further and further apart. My mother, also a Michael Jackson fan, went back to school, warning me to get over my obsession with Michael Jackson and take care of my baby. She became a nurse in the '70s and a new wife to a town family doctor who put us in a newer home in a flourishing neighborhood. Mother failed in her efforts to make me see that the light to prosperity was not sitting around the house having babies and waiting for Michael Jackson to enter my life.

I was the dark horse who sided with my father's tawdry affair only to remain defiant to my headstrong mother. Back then I found the simple life – being a dropout, marrying bad men, getting pregnant, and talking shit – easier than owning up to responsibility. I loved rebellion against a stepfather and I loved being challenged by two perfect brothers that proved education was my way out of my persistent ghetto mentality. In spite of the family encouragement, and my real father's slide downward, I stayed in defiance of doing better for myself by rejecting a good upbringing.

As low as my ambition was then, I knew if I hooked up with my idol, Michael Jackson, that my ambition would turn into determination and we'd succeed in love.

Michael and I were literally two ships in the night that belonged together on equal footing. Seeing him on TV were the happiest moments of my life. My obsession was beyond fanfare, yet I'd never approach him in any form. I believed 100% from the time I first laid eyes on him that Michael Jackson was mine.

Actually meeting him to forge our long life together would just happen in a matter of time. Our destiny was predetermined, and I had nothing to worry about in that regard. I believed that, so there was no reason to preempt my fate.

While hating on me may be a real possibility, I ain't lying about any of this, nor am I out to prove that I was really with Michael Jackson or that I am not a crazed fan. I have compassion and respect for you if you are one of the trillions of people in love with

Michael Jackson. I was about to get hooked up righteously into something that made going to college look so lame and so much like a waste of time.

Ain't thumbing my finger at education, but to love a man like Michael Jackson meant making incredible, abnormal sacrifices that most people could not have mastered. I had to keep my life free for the day that I'd meet him. It'd take a rare talent to deal with my bad behavior and my foul mouth and his enormous fame. I had to know when to cuss and when not to cuss, yet as a woman I had to hold down my man's interest, in spite of the bullshit that I witnessed happening around him.

I earned a doctorate in that thing called loving with discretion. No other couple I know could have made it through what Michael Jackson and I went through, because making the sacrifices had to be done for love and understanding. Since Mother never believed I'd hook this superstar anyway, Michael Jackson and I would attend her funeral in 1993 via Michael's two-million-dollar private jet without her ever knowing I was with the "Thriller." My brothers would be shocked into submission when they saw me enter the funeral side by side with Michael Jackson, for they'd see that all the money they spent on magazines and posters had been worth every dime. When they saw Michael decked out in a smooth black Fedora, wearing his familiar aviator sunglasses with fine black wool from the Gucci spring line with his trademark white socks and three-thousand-dollar black penny loafers, the entire Catholic congregation forgot about my 64-year-old mother in her baby-blue casket. Tim and Walt shook his hand in total disbelief. I'd kiss each brother, glad to see them both, and then I'd walk away with Michael by my side. Instead of asking questions, they were all stunned when they saw us carrying the European yellow and green wreath that Michael laid on my mother's closed casket. Michael saluted my mother, and then together we walked back to the wooden bench to sit with Tim and Walter.

Privately our love derived out of a deep dedication that we had for one another and our tantalizing ability to hide our love from the world. We thought it was real from "Gate Street." And it became surreal in life!

I loved Michael Jackson instantly. He was my high school diploma, my college degree, my certification to everlasting love. This love was wrapped in a careful package of understanding. Here is thanking God almighty for gifting this special man to me, only me. I had to accept his high life; he had to accept my low one. So that was the infinite formula that kept us together. At the end of the day, we protected each other perfectly.

Handlers would ask Michael, "Man, what the hell you see in Frankie Mae? The bitch goes off over the simplest things. She's lacking in every category, including looks. Her teeth ain't right. She's too thin and she ain't got any hair, and she thinks she's the most special person in your life, Michael."

"If Webster could put *ghetto* in the dictionary again, her picture would be on top of the word," an agent promised.

As funny as this may seem to haters, Michael didn't find a damn thing funny about agents slamming his babe, Frankie Mae. I came from good salt. But being upstanding always tasted damn funny to me. I mean, he was not having it when it came to anybody trying to clown me. I was there in '83 when he warned the agent. Suffice it to say the showdown over the pork ribs was not a pretty scene. This scene took place a week after "Billie Jean" and "Beat it" hit number one on the charts in the UK, and it was the same year Michael paid 47 million dollars for the rare Beatles music collection. Presenting then at the net worth of 70 million dollars, Michael Jackson was without a doubt at the peak of his wealth gain.

It was a hot spring night in San Francisco. I call it the night Michael Jackson went smooth off on the agent over me. Dressed in a simple white strapless dress I got from Sears, I did not match the finery of Michael Jackson in any way, and I never would 'cause I never tried. My feet always hurt because I stood up all day at work as a security guard.

So when Michael picked me up in his private jet for this dinner affair, I told him, "Wait, baby. Got to put something on my feet I can walk in." Michael was standing on that airstrip smiling at me as I reached in my dollar-store sack for a blue pair of Charter Club house shoes. I put them on. Next thing I knew I was sitting next to my man on his plane, and I wore them shoes to dinner that night, no problem.

Michael and I had agreed to eat at the Four Seasons

in San Francisco on Market Street. This beautiful hotel, situated in the Yerba Buena cultural district, was two blocks from Union Square, in the Financial District, near the Moscone Convention Center and the Museum of Modern Arts. Michael said he liked Four Seasons for its distinctive, luxurious experience and for all that San Francisco offers. On this notable evening we dined at this handsomely vibrant restaurant that featured the best in contemporary deco. Michael had arranged seating with special lighting effects and colorful artwork that was dramatically offset by dark blue Norwegian granite floors and hardwood finishes. Tonight Michael had arranged for us to dine in a private room that was ideal for entertaining up to eighteen guests, but tonight it was just the agent, Michael, me, and a few patrons scattered here and there. He had wanted to do something special just for me without all of the familiar fanfare that Michael was accustomed to. In typical form, tonight we were sitting at a luxurious table decked in vanilla white linen. As wonderful as this all sounds, the nice part of the evening ended with the décor.

I had to cuss the waitress out for bringing a plate of pork to my man that he did not order. The pretty blonde came in with some ghetto special instead of the seasonally changing vegetarian menu that is unique in the San Francisco steakhouse genre. Michael had allergies and was allergic to a lot of things. He hated pork. He'd always told me to keep pork out of his midst or get it off the table should his mind be on something else (which it usually was). The agent got out of line this night. Apparently, he had called the chef in advance for this greasy entrée without telling us. Now he was all up in my grill after I tore into the waitress over bringing that mess to the table. All I said to the girl was, "Bitch, my man don't eat this shit. Take it away."

The kind waitress understood "bitch" perfectly, as did Michael Jackson. Michael smiled at her approving my order when she picked that silver tray up over her pretty bouncy curls and got ghost white as she took it away from the table. My man rubbed my thigh, thanking me for looking out for his interests as he sipped one of his favorite Calera wines. I was ever so proud.

But that uppity agent – that big, bulky nigga who was completely out of the loop – came out of the fucking bag. I mean, he acted like such a fool all up in this nice ass restaurant that my man had no choice but to put his ass in check on the spot.

"Frankie Mae, you don't talk to people that way!" the agent shouted, referring to my calling the waitress a bitch earlier. "There is a proper way to address people without calling them 'bitch,' he complained.

Nobody paid attention to his sneaky ass. When my man didn't say a thing about it, he appealed his case directly to Michael. "Man, can you tell her to get some class?" the agent warned. Sitting next to Michael, I knew the agent was in trouble when Michael, perfectly groomed from his recent "Thriller" promotion, dressed in a beautiful black leather jumpsuit and steel-toed Armani boots, motioned that nigga aside, with nothing short of class.

"Can I have a word with you, Agent?" Michael asked, quietly. The place was crowded now. All the white folks with their little white hands placed neatly on the white tablecloths used diplomacy as they politely cleared the way for the crying waitress who was running away from our table with a tray that was dripping with red pork ribs. None of them needed to have a clue what was about to happen. The agent responded to Michael's request. He rose from his seat, tossing me a dirty look, while at the same time my man gave me an adoring, reassuring smile.

Michael was so mad at the agent – he didn't leave the polished walnut table. He gently grabbed the agent's arm right there from across the elegant round table. He gritted his teeth, holding back some fire when he let the shocked agent have it.

"You ordered that crap knowing we don't eat pork, Agent. Don't blame her for fixing that. Frankie means everything to me. What the hell is wrong with you? You should know how I feel about this woman by now. She defended me; don't you ever open your mouth to say a cross thing about my woman or question her judgment again. You understand that?" He dropped the agent's arm and took a deep breath, his chest pounding through all that prime black leather.

After a long stare-down with the agent, Michael then turned to the nosy crowd. With that he smiled and waved to all of his fans inside that restaurant, as though he had taken his stand only to acknowledge the onlookers. The crowd clapped at Michael's kind gesture, one sweep of his famous gloved hand, never getting a clue of what was really going on. Obligingly Michael nodded as he quietly placed his right hand on my shoulder for unending support. His touch quieted me for the rest of the night.

Soon five waiters came to the beautiful gold-lit round table with gold and rust colored *Vegetarian* menus secured especially for Michael. He chose one menu and then used his diamond-studded Marc Anthony cell phone to call his chef to come assist the one on duty and prepare his proper meal. He then handed the menu to me, while the agent settled for dreaming about eating those pork-filled red baby back ribs.

"Baby, do you mind selecting a meatless spinach quiche for us?" Michael Jackson asked.

"Not at all, *dahling*," I teased, pretending to manufacture the class the agent thought I was lacking. The agent glared at me with hateful fury in his eyes, and then in typical form, when he couldn't stay mad much longer, he reached out to shake Michael's hand and we all broke out laughing. "You can have a seat now," Michael reminded the man kindly. Michael quieted that agent just as easily as he had hiked that nigga into check place.

"Man, call that fine waitress back over here, and brother, you go on and eat your greasy pork ribs," Michael joked.

We laughed the whole night over the incident.

Having nothing more to say to Michael Jackson about me, the agent ended up getting his ribs, and I mean that greedy nigga took *grub* to a whole new level, slopping up all that pork. And every time he looked at us he shook his head with thick grease dripping everywhere and I died laughing at his ghetto ass.

So you see, Michael Jackson loved his Frankie Mae, bad or good, and this was something many of his handlers found hard to take; but in time they'd all get used to me after my man got through checking them. With my knack for simplicity and spontaneity to cuss people out, I was about as abnormal as you were going to get; yet Michael Jackson knew me like a road map and he often told me he loved me because I was exactly the woman he needed in his life at this time. No doubt he knew I was a smart chick who liked my ghetto on ice. My man reminded me of my mother the way he could toss you a look that would have you dodging for cover.

People had to recognize that when it came to Frankie Mae, you could take the girl out of the ghetto, but the ghetto could not leave me. I was his one and only ghetto love who would never change. I was his head-bobbing, Kool-Aid-loving, raggedy ass, sailor-talking, and Tootsie Roll Pop-eating sugar momma. That night he kissed me passionately at the dinner table in front of the agent and all those prissy white folks to a round of great applause. When the waitress came back later to clear the table, she offered me her hand personally to apologize for her mistake.

You're going to crack up later when you see what happened to Grace, so stick around. Grace was a handler who thought Michael's ugly ghetto girl was a little too loud, and too ghetto for the likes of the world entertainer. This happened after he got burned filming that Pepsi commercial. As the agent learned when he bad mouthed Michael's ghetto girl, Frankie Mae had the means to cause you to get checked and or be fired by Michael Jackson.

Say What

The real Michael Jackson was more than just the "King of Pop," or any of that other stuff they called him. Michael was something powerful. He was so beautiful that to love him in person was something out of this world. To me, everything about him was purely magical. Without being an entertainer, Michael Jackson was a very fine man who dressed like a king.

In terms that the world will clearly understand, you can't get something you don't know. Number one: Michael J. Jackson was not a child abuser – period – and all of his time with my kids and me included donating money to charities and trying to help people. This man loved my children more purely than their own fathers did. Loving them had nothing to do with money. Michael cared.

Ladies, I know your mouths are open just waiting for this next line. I'm a give it to you now, so sit your ol' nasty asses down and let me give it to you straight the way I know you like it.

THE LOVE HE SAVED

Michael was an excellent lover! Yes to God he was. Okay, the thing you saw on TV with Lisa Marie – the kiss was not real and even little Lisa Marie Presley was in on that one. That's not said to hate on the love she showed Thursday, September 3, 2009, when they hauled my man's gold casket into that mausoleum and she cried; now that was real. I give my props to Lisa Marie for showing Michael love during crucial times in his life. Lisa Marie Presley is my girl. She is one of those kinds of people who will never turn her back on a friend. Married or not, Michael was her friend to the end. I got you on that, girl, and the world feels your pain. I was sitting near Janet Jackson when it happened.

But let's be real. How could that shit be real (the kiss) when the man so loved me? He was the smartest entertainer the world would ever know, yet he was shy. He was not about to put his best hooks out there like that on live TV. He was innocent, and he was as average as the day is long. Motivated by intense privacy and normalcy, he loved me, he loved my kids, he loved his family, he loved his father Joseph just as much as he loved his mother Katherine . . . so there, Nancy Grace.

POW! I have pretty much told you the whole story, but I ain't through yet. Keep going; I give it to your ass on the rocks, bitch style, the way I know you like it. Don't believe everything you read in the media; but believe all that I am telling you here. All those words ain't true about Michael being on the wrong side of the right. The Michael Jackson I knew and loved saved the most precious part of his love for me, and y'all – even the haters – can just take that.

~~~

I want to tell you how I met Michael Jackson and found out firsthand that he was a lover of the world. He was the most effective, most sincere caretaker of my heart. I met him in the early '80s while I was still a young woman, but the recognition came mostly from Michael Jackson. There was never a day that I could not believe the world's greatest entertainer truly had saved his heart for me. He told me it was a storefront picture that did the trick, making him fall in love with me. Remember this; I had so many pictures of Michael Jackson on my wall, and my mother made me tear them all down. He saw me only weeks after I had innocently flirted into the camera of a broke, unknown photographer who was intent on turning a lonely, newly hired security guard with a jacked attitude and a broken front tooth into a model, if only for one day. My life-changing day in a dying San Francisco photo shop happened like this:

"Be still, little girl. Fix your neck. This is my last roll of film," the French cameraman declared. "You have no money. You're not a pretty girl at all, but I can make you look like something if you will only be still. If you're a good girl, I'll get a great shot for the window so the whole world will see you. Who knows who will see the picture!"

I just so happens that in his heyday he shot Clark Gable, Rita Hayworth, Susan Hayward, and other huge Hollywood stars. But that day he had fallen on hard times and was just one shot away from ending his
~~~

career. On a brisk, cold evening inside a dusty studio, in front of fading yellow lights that flickered off and on, the photographer and I both wanted only one thing: to get the perfect still shot.

I had posed for Rodolfo Almeria as a glib eighteen-year-old who had just come to the city to get a job as a security guard. The following day I'd be placed at the front desk of a department store in Oakland, California, where I would work for many years. It just so happened I was trying out a new blonde hairstyle and I wanted to take a picture of it because the hair to me was just so tight. I was wearing the same hairstyle you see on this book cover. Nobody could tell that Elmo – my husband of the time – had just beaten me for breakfast, leaving knots in my head.

"Bitch, you look like hell in that wig," he said to me. I thought I looked great, hiding the signs of his physical abuse to my head.

Today I was blonde, young, and fresh as hell. I was going to prove to that raving mad husband that I was somebody. Fascinated by the beautiful clothes people could wear during photo sessions, I couldn't wait for the cameraman to shoot me his prop in a nice gray sweater with a simple white pearl around my neck. Then, holding back the tears of a beating that ended my marriage, I turned my cute, sore head high over my right shoulder, just like that French photographer man told me to.

Afterwards, I went home, never thinking again

about that photo shoot. I got into bed, never telling my abusive husband about the simulated class picture photo that would one day catch the eyes of one of the world's most incredible entertainers and change my entire life.

A Picture Is Worth a Second Look

Who knew when I gleaned a smile, hiding my chipped gold tooth perfectly, that Michael Jackson would see this photo and then fall in love with me forever? It was a photo I took wishing I had not dropped out of high school to have a baby. It was a picture I wished Elmo had seen to save our failing marriage. It was a picture that would change lives.

Michael Jackson and I became engaged in the '80s at the height of Michael's career. Our engagement was not ceremonious in the conventional sense. Our engagement meant creating and keeping a connection that would survive the ages. While the media questioned his race, his manhood, and his sexuality, my brother would be rocking the hell out of me in bed, while I wanted to do a drive-by on the haters, for real. I would be there for Michael Jackson in this life in ways you'd never imagine. Not knowing his heart created a safe haven for a love affair that would have truly rocked the nation.

~~~

I met him on the Santa Monica freeway in the early
~~~

'80s one sunny evening after signing the papers with my lawyer on a nasty divorce. I had stopped in Santa Monica for a hamburger and some fries to fulfill my mother's wish for me to put my new divorce behind me and pick up a few pounds. The stress of a two-year abusive marriage and a cold divorce caused weight loss that needed intervention. To make my mother happy, I even ate a slice of apple pie with ice cream at Denny's before jumping into my old beat-up silver and brown '70s model Nissan Maxima to head back up north to my new apartment and my new job as a security guard in Oakland, California.

Recently divorced, there was nothing to hurry back to except a job as a security guard at a department store and two starving, cute little boys who I loved with all my motherly heart. By my mid-twenties I had been married twice already. The first to Elmo ended early when my twenty-year-old husband died of heart disease just a week after he beat me for taking the class photo. The last one ended over my husband beating me all the time – I had my tubes tied on his ass.

Now I was swearing off relationships for good, as I felt lucky to get out of marriages, period. A young woman with two kids and a messed-up job – I felt washed up and was sure no man in his right mind would ever want me. Suddenly it was back to high school all over again. Average looking with a tiny frame that sometimes made me look like a child, I felt my life was pretty much boring and over. Who knew a few minutes into this ride of destiny that *he* would roll down the black-tinted window of a stretch limousine to pull me over and change my boring ghetto life forever, over an old class photo he saw and fell in love with that literally had no class?

"Hey, Frankie Mae," yes you in the San Francisco window! I can't believe it's really you!" he shouted, like I was the goddamn star he knew all his life. Yeah, I had written a few kitchen table books when I was lonely on my job as a security guard. I published a few thinking I was a good writer. I never thought anything I wrote would catch a reading light. Most of what I wrote was about my abusive childhood and marriages. I had even penned love stories that had no legs. At first I kept driving, headed eagerly back up north to the Bay Area, as I was stunned that this star actually knew me by name.

In case you're asking how I knew him . . . Of course I knew who he was. Hell, it was Michael Jackson. No sense pretending or setting this up like I was star-struck or something. Hell, I had loved this man, this nigga, my whole damn ass life. I would have left either one of my husband's for him just like anybody else with good sense. I had rehearsed everything I'd do if I ever met him for real. This was my nigga no matter how white his skin got.

My mother and father knew his family in the '60s. We were from Gary, Indiana. I had dreamed of him in high school since "The Love You Save." My dreams were the kind of dreams you don't ever want to wake up from. While high school friends wanted Marlon, Jackie, Jermaine, or Tito, even Randy, I wanted Michael Jackson. He was three years younger than I, but I knew he'd catch up to my age one day, and hell, ol' Frankie Mae was gonna be waiting for her man.

Only problem was I didn't look the way I wanted to look this Saturday at 4:00 pm on the Santa Monica freeway. To be honest, I ain't ever looked the way I wanted to look. I looked like a dope addict or a drunk, but I never was either. I damn sure knew if I ever saw this man in person, I was going to reel his ass in, good hair day or not. I had always loved the King of Pop since those damn Osmond brothers made "One Bad Apple," trying to be like them. That song started a fistfight at Garey High School in Pomona, California – early '70s, mind you. One friend went home to put razorblades in her hair for the publicized afterschool fight. Nevelin was going to kick my ass after sixth period for getting the Jacksons wrong. It was on over Michael Jackson. I have always loved Michael and I think Nevelin loved him more than I did back in the day. Discussing music or entertainers always caused fights at school, especially if you had your facts wrong. I was ready to fight over "One Bad Apple," insisting it was the Jacksons. Sherry said it was not the Jacksons and I had better check my ass or I was gonna get my ass kicked. I said it was the Jacksons to all three of them hos.

"Bitch, I'm a kick yo' ass over not knowing your music," I was told by Nevelin. I said it was the Jacksons again. It took going to the record store to end this argument. This was before you could just check shit out on the Internet. It took running five miles down Garey

Avenue on a blistering hot day, miles away from school to confirm shit, or girls with razorblades in their hair were going to kick your ass. I ran into the record store looking for John Groove, the record store man. He told me "One Bad Apple" was the Osmonds and that revelation meant it was my ass with Nevelin and the other hos. That was the day I dropped out of school. I never wanted to look those bitches in the eyes again! I loved Michael Jackson too damn much to get a song wrong.

Never in my wildest dreams did I ever expect to be on the same street with the King of Pop, Michael Jackson. It was a very hot day, about three hours before sundown. This limo kept coming closer and closer. The freeway was jam-packed. This was before cell phones and I was bugging like hell to tell somebody – anybody – about the fact that Michael Jackson was flirting with me. The ones who I wanted to see most were those jealous hos from high school. This was the day them bitches would have given Frankie Mae her props.

Sweat poured down the sides of my face. Suddenly I was glad my family pushed for my divorce. Both my lawyer brothers got me through this even though I was terrified to be alone. I thanked them for saving my life as I turned the radio off and just kept on driving, hoping that this superstar was the fuck for real on this one. This was like being in a nightclub. I was bouncing all crazy in the seat of an old broken-down car, ghetto style, getting down with a group called the Ohio Players. And that car, already on its last legs, wasn't having it. I was snapping, shaking, popping – hitting all the moves well enough to be in one of Michael Jackson's videos. I was showing my ass big time, knowing that nigga was checking my ass out.

You know how it is when you're looking at a fine guy. Then you notice he's standing at the wall not trying to hit on anybody because he's too fine. You have to be the perfect chick before this guy is going to talk to you. Otherwise you got to play the man's role and hit on his ass. Then, out of nowhere, right when you get up the nerve to go over there, you see him coming. At first you think he's going to talk to your good-looking girlfriend with the light skin, the blue eyes, and the long black hair, and what the hell, that nigga with his fine ass walked right past that girl and he's rolling over to talk to you? You say to yourself, *Oh no he didn't.* Then you look again at the surprise on your fine friend's face and realize, *Oh yes he did!*

Well, ladies, that's the same way I was feeling at that moment just minutes before Michael Jackson became mine.

I had it going on and there was no competition to hate on this. There was no Sherry or Nevelin making me run down to the store to prove or verify shit. There was no bitch with razorblades in her hair that was going to contest this union going down! And thank God there was no Halle Berry-looking bitch trying to pick up my man on the strength.

If only this old raggedy-ass car was a tight red Ford Mustang with Rouse rims, tinted windows, a booming sound system, and all the hookups, I'd be tight as hell.

However, even without all that, this was a dream. Even with my car ditching in and out of traffic, needing a front wheel alignment, I took one hand off the steering wheel, powering that mother with the other to keep my cool on. The car rolled damn near into the front seat of Michael's limo and I thought I was done. I mean, I saw him good this time. I pinched myself with this messed-up car screeching loudly until the driver behind me, some old-ass black man, started yelling, causing the whole freeway to launch into a horn-blowing match. It was a hot day, and horns were beeping and people acting all crazy over what that crazy man started.

"Keep that damn raggedy hoopty straight, or get that piece of weaving shit off the road, you ugly-ass bitch," he shouted. "Get off the road!"

I'm thinking, *Nigga, you ain't gonna mess up my getting with Michael over a damn wrong lane change.* It was on now. I was happier than I had ever been in my life. I was about to get the hookup for real with this nigga calling me all kinds of ugly bitches. I was feeling this superstar and I knew by the way he kept rolling down that tinted window in that fancy car he was all up into feeling my black ass, too. Today, right now, he was my nigga on the wall, off the wall, however you wanna call it!

That beautiful, fine, mocha-colored, singing-and-can-dance-his-ass-off brother with a well-coiffed Jherri curl of perfectly curved baby hair framing the sides of his pretty face was shouting out of his car at me the same time some old-ass nigga was calling me names.

While Michael Jackson was waving me down, Mr. Trying To Spoil Everything paced to go ahead of me. My Lord! Out of fright, I yanked my car back into my lane, letting the old grumpy cock-blocker go ahead in front of me.

For the third time Michael Jackson rolled down his window. Now he was singing to me loudly. With both his hands cupped around his thin lips, he shouted across lanes, "Pretty young thing, repeat after me. Say now, now, now!" He pulled me over, and shoot I wanted to say, "Now, now, now," but that was foolish. He was guiding me off the freeway to a nearby exit. Once we got this car thing in safer territory, he introduced himself.

"I'm Michael Jackson," he said, standing with me on the driver's side of my ugly car.

"Nigga, I know who the fuck you are. Are you crazy? So you don't even have to go there with me!"

Michael put his hands over his mouth, not believing how badly I talked. He smiled at me. I could see the stars in his eyes.

"Nigga," I continued, "I almost got my ass kicked over an Osmond song because of you. I ain't never gonna forget your fine ass!"

"Really?" he asked, surprised. He was standing there looking good as hell, I mean. Much taller than his photos, Michael had that lure about him that all women look for in a man. He was sexy as all hell today. The powers of who he was and the allure of how great he looked made me feel comfortable.

At first I was afraid to stop for the huge black limousine that had spent all those minutes shouting and singing to me. Now, I looked around the freeway, seeing motorists who recognized the entertainer. I was stunned he was standing here talking to me, little ol' Frankie Mae from Gary, Indiana.

Motorists began hollering to the star that stood next to me alongside the road. "Michael, Michael," they screamed. I was standing there freezing. I couldn't believe this was really happening to me.

People were driving up to stop and take a look at the world's most famous entertainer. I was a divorced mother of two hoping I'd make it back up north in a few hours to fix dinner – some pork and beans and wieners for my kids. Then I was going to hand-wash my guard uniform for work tomorrow and haul my ass into bed. Naw, I didn't look all that great and I never wore makeup. Earlier I had torn my bob weave out. Girls, you know how we tear out the weave when it gets to itching. It still looked good, but now I'm thinking I could have left it in one more day. Hell, I told my mother nobody was gonna see me, so I tore the shit out, washed my hair, and you know the rest. I let my short hair go natural, wishing for fullness to set in that never did. That normally takes about a week to be just right.

Now my fly-away strands made me look like a

cancer victim. Michael tirelessly signed autographs on the dangerous freeway, while he noticeably kept one eye on me. I pulled my hand through my hair, but it wasn't working for me. Through the light wind, my hair fought back with its own form of electricity. I had a gold frame around my front right tooth that made me look like the lady version of Lil Wayne. I was sure he'd get a better look at me and be gone.

But, strangely, Michael Jackson liked me. I was standing there doing everything I could to make myself look pretty for a man I had loved my whole young life. Beautiful models, great-looking men, and people of all races held Michael up for two hours on that freeway until a highway patrolman ended the autograph session, and not once did he show interest in anyone but me.

Hours later, he pulled me closer to his chest. He helped me when he ran his hands through my thin hair, killing my style completely. "Thanks for being so patient and letting me do that for the fans," he said. "You have the prettiest skin I have ever seen. I like it that you don't have any makeup on and that you're a little rough around the edges. Your eyes are a sweet, soft brown."

I was shocked into silence. Michael told me we were going to go and I could leave the car on the side of the road for a tow truck. We made it to his incredible limo, and that car was one for the books. It had a twenty-passenger red and black seating design, six plasma TV screens, two DVD players, a laser show of Michael's latest videos, fiber optic and neon lighting, and a JBL sound system that lit up the entire freeway with the blasting sound of "I'll be There." Michael pulled me into the beautiful luxury VIP area that was marked with his diamond-studded initials.

"Are these diamonds real?"

"Of course they're real. Girl, the way that thing swings so wide in those lanes, you could really hurt yourself." We laughed about my old car.

"I'll send you a brand new car tomorrow," he promised, as I ogled the luxury of his driving environment in awe.

Later inside the car, his driver gave me a Coke with ice in one of the largest tumblers I had ever seen. I held the cup branded with Michael's initials in complete shock. He looked even more amazing in person! I couldn't wait to tell my young sons, Shuun and Daryle, about meeting Michael Jackson today. He looked sexy with his fresh, black Jherri curl framing his beautiful mocha skin and his wide, dark eyes. He was more regal in person than he was on TV. With his hair pulled back in a cute ponytail, I was immediately turned on by Michael's impeccable manners. I had sworn off men, but now the light was turned on brightly, and I was already planning the wedding, never once considering that Michael Jackson would ever leave me.

As I eased closer to Michael, the crowds had gotten a whiff of what was going on. Some even checked out the beat-up Nissan, trying to guess what was going on, and others followed our long car. Michael rolled down the tinted window to look at the fans. Together we laughed heartily as he told the driver to turn up the heater and drive faster. With my hair completely flat, I felt like a queen in his regal presence. Because of the way Michael looked at me, I was beautiful then. It was the early '80s and I was in my prime. I was a dark chocolate, 112-pound ghetto rat with bad language and a worse attitude, but on this day I had truly felt love, beauty, and happiness, all at the same time. Being in Michael Jackson's presence quieted me down in ways I had never experienced before. How many people can say, "I'm riding in the limo with Michael Jackson?" Life simply does not get any better than that!

"I could feel you from the back of this car," Michael said to me. I was shocked into speechlessness. He eased closer to me.

"Before you ask me about the gold tooth . . ." I defended.

"Let me guess," he offered, flashing that classic smile that had framed so many magazines and TV screens. His teeth were so pretty I started counting them one by one. When he spoke, his sound was soothing, gentle, and precise; his diction was the best I had ever heard. I was beyond crazy when I smiled at him as he told a story about me that was shockingly accurate.

"I hope you don't mind me turning up the heater. You were so cold out there when I was signing autographs. I couldn't wait to get you in the car and give you some heat," he said. His thoughtful gesture showed me how kind and considerate Michael Jackson was. Star-struck, I wanted nothing more than just to be in his presence for life.

"You were a cute little girl playing outside with your two brothers in Gary, Indiana," he chimed. The limo driver closed the diamond-trimmed glass divider to give us privacy. I leaned into Michael as he told me a story about how I lost my chipped front tooth.

"You were all so excited. You played ball freely like children always do. And, you were at your grandmother's house, too," he said excitedly. "Then your brother, we'll call him Richard, tossed the ball to you. You weren't looking, were you?"

"No, I wasn't looking at all," I confirmed.

"That's why the ball hit you in the mouth, huh? You lost only part of your tooth, but not the whole thing," he said innocently. I watched Michael tell me this story with tears in his eyes. Youth and childhood memories meant a great deal to him. As if I had known him his whole life, I wanted the story to be his way. I could tell he needed this. Fantasy was something he and I both needed. We were on our way to fulfilling each other's needs.

"That night, your grandmother came into your room while you were asleep," he continued excitedly. "She put a shiny nickel under your pillow. She always gave you shiny nickels, huh?" I agreed by nodding yes, as I wanted to scream out my happiness of being with him. "When you got home, your father – one of my father's old work friends – took you to the dentist. And that is how you got that beautiful, gold ghetto tooth."

After Michael's story, we both laughed so hard we wanted to pee. First he laughed, and then I laughed, with my hands covering the tooth he described. I had never had such an innocent, sweet time with a guy ever.

Whereas I was quiet and completely star-struck, Michael had a lot to say to me about everything, even *Thriller*. He told me that album was going to break all records and revolutionize the entire music industry. At the mention of *Thriller* I was about to faint as I remembered a time when my father told my family about his father's wish to see them become successful. Our paths had crossed before, but I had never met Michael Jackson in person. No need faking what Michael meant to me. If I never saw him again after that day, I'd cherish this moment. I'd do something very rare. I'd spend each minute with Michael, showing love and respecting him as a man who valued the innocence in everyday human beings.

Soon we were farther away from Los Angeles and my old abandoned Nissan Maxima. The beautiful sunset was turning into dark. Drivers who had formerly spent a great deal of effort trying to peek into the fancy limousine, completed their turnoffs to resume their lives. Having been rid of the excited fans, Michael tapped on the tinted glass behind the driver's seat, telling him to head straight up to the place where he first saw me in San Francisco, California. We continued to talk, as we never ran out of things to say. A few hours into the drive, the King of Pop kissed me gently on the right cheek. I closed my eyes, then opened them, dizzy from being in love.

"Frankie Mae, after you get out of this car I may not see you up close like this again for a very long time. Please remember this day," he said, gently lifting my chin to his famous, beautiful face.

"No matter what you hear about me, what you see on TV, or what I shall become, I love you, Frankie Mae. I know it's kind of soon," he defended, holding up his famous hand, "but I'm for real." Not knowing what to say, we shared a long glance at one another. My heart began to beat over my chest as this lovely entertainer leaned slowly down to meet my face with the gift of a well-approached kiss. As I felt the heat of his breath arouse me, I rolled the window down to a flashbulb from the paparazzi. It surprised me how close they could get to a car that was in motion. Soon, I quickly rolled the window all the way up. Michael was not the least bit phased about the man who had tried to steal a bit of our privacy.

"Sorry. I should have told you about that," he said, referring to the paparazzi.

"About what..The price of fame?" I asked.

"You got it, kiddo!" he chimed. We laughed heartily again.

I gently placed my lips back up to Michael's for another dream-filled kiss. And then I kissed him long and passionately for dear life. Though thin, his body was very strong. His lips were full and soft as he defied what people said about his sexuality in the mass media. And, as he kissed me, I felt the insatiable need of a man. I appreciated the beautiful story he gave me about the history of my ugly gold tooth, and all I wanted to do now was please him. The minute I released my mouth from his, the gold tooth fell into my lap. I was so embarrassed that I had not glued it in as I normally do. I didn't know what to say to him about this. It happened so awkwardly I couldn't hide it.

Unmoved by the chipped tooth, Michael Jackson pressed his mouth back to mine to let me know he could never get enough of my pure love. He promised to protect me, saying he'd never judge me or even let others judge me. His simplicity and his warm love for the world proved he would never expect me to be perfect, for he loved me just the way I was. Next, he talked as if he had known me my whole life. I was shocked at what came later.

Michael had the driver go all the way up north to San Francisco to Market Street. Hours later, he asked the driver, a man I would come to know well as "Agent," to stop at a window that presented to the world an old photo of me from the '70s. It was the one I had posed for, trying to be a model for just one day after friends ran me away from school in shame over not knowing Michael Jackson's songs. My hair was in the Farrah Fawcett style (short version). I was laid out in a cute beige sweater with a white pearl placed around my neck. I had tried feverishly to hide the gold tooth. I was indeed successful. The picture was so cute – the photographer had put it in the window years ago, just as he had promised. The red brick store was boarded up completely except for the photo.

When we arrived at the window, Michael asked me to get out of the car. Next, he excitedly raced up to the dusty window with me. Together we were like children as we got our hands dirty clearing away the dust from the large, forgotten storefront window. Michael was just seconds away from verifying the photo was me.

"Is that you?" he asked, waiting for my answer. "Please tell me that's you," he begged, pointing to the eighteen-year-old fresh version of me. Tears began to fill my eyes as I remembered all the pain I had been hiding while taking this photo. To tell the truth, I was glad the picture was me. If it had been somebody else, my ass was grass. To imagine him leaving me over a photo that was not me was mind-boggling.

I bowed my head, feeling lucky the picture was me and feeling sad that I had never really graduated from high school. The picture did not belong to a class. The picture was to me a mere fulfillment of lost dreams of pain. I was able to put the gold tooth back together while he wasn't looking.

"Yes, that is me," I shyly answered back. I stood in front of the window, cold, rocking side to side, wondering what in the hell was wrong with Michael Jackson for liking me. That picture was black and white. It was ten years old, and to me I looked like somebody's lost puppy.

"You're crying?" he asked gently, as he came closer to wipe away my tears.

"I'm okay," I said, letting him dry my tears.

"I am indeed a lucky man!" he pronounced, lifting my chin gently. "You don't have to cry." He placed his other gloved hand on my shoulder. "You remind me a lot of my little sister Janet," he said happily. I was glad Janet didn't hear what he said. Janet was beautiful. My God, what was Michael Jackson thinking? Had he lost his mind?

"Does she have a chipped gold tooth?" I asked him.

Michael laughed heartily, "of course not, Frankie Mae. You are so cute." He pulled me to his side. "Janet's my little sister. Your eyes are a soft brown like hers. You're a little brash. But you look kind of shy like her."

I smiled at the compliment, thinking Michael had lost his damn mind. I loved it. I loved watching his sister Janet on *Good Times* and I remembered crying when she played the abused child Penny on the show.

"You have round cheeks and chocolate, beautiful, clear skin like Janet, my mother, and my sister, Rebbie.

Frankie Mae, I have been trying to find you ever since the day I first saw that picture of you two years ago. I saw it with one of my brothers and I kept saying to the driver. 'Stop the car!'

"I looked for who you were, and back then the most I could come up with was your beautiful name, Frankie Mae. I called photographers everywhere. Nobody could tell me who you were or where you lived. I did everything but put out a PSA to find you," he declared in the softest, sweetest voice I had ever heard.

We were back in the car now. His driver nodded his head up and down in assent, while I marveled at how this innocent event had drawn in a huge crowd. Michael, dressed in a red and gold fedora, wearing a beautiful black leather vest and pants to match, ignored the crowd this time. He began talking to me as if nobody was there. I could feel the heat of the people shouting his name.

"Hey, it's Michael Jackson, everybody. It's him, live!" a person shouted. As the crowd began to swell, Michael continued talking to me as if we were the only people on the street at the stoplight. The agent got out of the car to deal with the crowd and keep them at bay. Wanting a concert, that crowd launched into Michael's early hits. They were dancing on Market Street in San Francisco while the King of Pop kept his focus on me.

"When I saw you in the little Nissan today, I never thought for a minute that it wasn't you. I have loved you since seeing your cute model photo in that shop here in San Francisco, and if you don't believe me you can ask my brother," he promised. "It was a lot of months ago, maybe years. I was leaving one of my attorneys' offices when my brother noticed how cute your picture was. I just happened to look out the window to see your photo. I could not turn away. My heart sank so quickly I had to get out of the car. Next, I raced into the abandoned shop to take the picture out of the window before new panes were installed. As you can see today, that never happened. He asked me if I wanted the picture and of course I said yes. I never forgot your beautiful name, Frankie Mae," he said sweetly. "And to see you in that car was a dream come true for me, because there is not a day that goes by when I don't think of your beautiful photo."

Michael kept me close to him as he blindly signed autographs for droves of fans who had literally left their cars to come up to ours to get his autograph. I was stunned. That anybody would remember the photo was shocking enough. But for that person to be Michael Jackson – I was stunned to silence.

From that moment on, both Michael and I cried. He signed autographs and he hugged me while he was doing it. I wanted to tell him that I fell in love with him back in the '70s when I was just sixteen years old – only two years before his favorite picture of me was born. I wanted to tell him so much about the other side of his fan love and how my mother begged me to take all of his pictures down and grow up. I wanted to tell him about Linda Floyd and Cherry Ann Gibson and

Phyllis Harris and how we raced to John Groove's record store to buy his 45s all the time. But my heart was so filled with love and joy that the past was trivial compared to being with him in real life. Today all I could do was love my man and be glad that he discovered and remembered me enough to spot me in an old car on a busy freeway. I hoped that we'd one day be together forever.

Later on Market Street, we were tucked back into privacy inside the impressive limousine.

"Do you want to come and live with me, you and the kids?" Michael asked me.

I thought about it for a second. I laughed seeing my little boy playing with Bubbles. And then I agreed right away that the answer would be yes. I knew that I could never pull this off in reality, but for this moment the answer was yes.

"I will take you home. I will send a jet for you in two days. Sell all of your belongings. You and Shuun and Daryle are coming home with me," Michael shouted, gleefully. There was certainly nothing to argue about. This was the man I had loved all of my life. I had always told people I'd be with Michael Jackson one day, and according to what he was telling me today, he loved me back.

Before Michael left me for the evening, he asked his driver to take us to a secret location where we ended up in a very private place where there were no fans begging for autographs. When the driver got out of the car, Michael became very serious with me. I shall never forget the words Michael Jackson spoke to me on this very special evening. He sat in the alleyway, with me sitting on his strong lap. I placed my head gently on his shoulder as a cool breeze whipped my thin strands against the beautiful hair framing his face.

"Frankie Mae, I plan to live the rest of my life with you and the children – be it here or afar. But remember this. If anything gets in our way between now and the time we get together, I will always love you, and only you. Don't change. Forget what people will say about your natural style. Remain who you are," he said, emphasizing those words. He stroked the sides of my face. My hair was a complete mess. I had stopped trying to comb it hours ago. In this surreal, quiet moment, Michael intuitively felt my insecurity about my looks. What he said was key to how comfortable I would feel when I was around him.

"I wear enough wigs and makeup for the both of us. Be you. Believe in me. I always tell people that all you have to do is believe. Unless you hear something directly from my lips, consider it unfounded, and don't believe it, Frankie Mae. If you see me with somebody and it's not you, then it's just something this earthly life expects me to do and it is not love."

Michael kissed me gently. I closed my eyes, enjoying it as his manhood began to rise beneath my blue jeans. As he talked, I placed my thin arms around his neck like in high school. I wanted him to talk. I wanted to hear all that he had to say.

"If the media accuses me of abandoning love, they will be referencing something they will never understand. I will never abandon these moments, I promise. If I change, it's because I can't get to you, Frankie Mae. You will always be the lady of my life."

Touched by the sincerity in Michael Jackson's voice, I began to cry happy tears. Suddenly all the abuse I had suffered in failed marriages was worth it to get to this moment. Somehow his beautiful story of how I broke my front tooth was the most beautiful story I had ever heard, no matter how far away from the truth it was. I'd never tell him that my mother knocked my tooth out with her fist. I would never, ever forget the time I spent with Michael Jackson. After he spoke his words so carefully to me, I was just as passionate during my turn.

"Michael, don't say these things to me if you don't mean it. I am very sensitive. I was abused as a child like you, and to tell you the truth, I don't know when I may fly off the handle and go off. When I hear stuff like you're telling me, baby, I get worried that I will not be able to please you if you don't please me. I will embarrass you one day and you will never forget it."

"You should take what I am telling you seriously, Frankie Mae. I am a man and if I can't control my little wild woman, then that's on me. If you embarrass me, I will handle that as a man, baby. Loving a woman means teaching your woman the things she needs to know to be stronger in the relationship," he advised.

"Nobody has ever said these kinds of things to me before," I said.

"Ah baby, you deserve love, just believe. No other man will love you the way I do. I have to be honest with you. I had some people research you. Yes, I knew who you were. I knew about your marriages and I just didn't want to interfere with anything. I could tell by the way he treated you, your marriage would be over one day. Meeting you had to be natural. How much more natural can this be?" Then he admitted, "I even know about the marital abuses."

"Oh, Michael," I stated, shocked.

"You say 'Oh, Michael' so cute," he said. "That's the only thing you've really said all day. I was beginning to think that somewhere along the line I had lost you, Frankie Mae."

"You could never lose me, Michael. I know this is all happening really fast. But I will always have your back no matter what I have to do, and I can explain the marriages. Don't you know who you are, Michael? Don't you see the impact you have on the world and how many people just want a piece of you, my love?"

I waited for him to stretch his legs out and get comfortable again before I tossed him the zinger.

"And then you go and hook up with a toothless security guard?"

We laughed again. This time we laughed real hard, and I didn't have to be a rocket scientist to see that Michael Jackson needed laughter.

"My God," he said, "Frankie Mae, don't ever say bad things about yourself to me again. Promise me you won't," he pleaded, sitting me back on top of his lap. Instead of answering back, I gave him a sorrowful look he understood immediately.

After a few moments of silence, he said, "No other woman in the world calls me Michael Jackson the way you do, Frankie Mae. You really understand me. That's why I feel you so closely. Your picture was more than just a snapshot; it's the most natural photo – all black and white – I have ever seen. I read your book, *What Happened to Suzy*. It was horrible what you went through. You knew I dressed up how you lost your tooth to make it funny so you'd laugh. There is never anything funny about being abused. You really are good at just going with the flow, and those boys Cornell and Darnell will get a gift for leaving you alone for me. I know your father was as bad, if not worse, than Joseph. But I know you love him because he's your father, like I love my father. That doesn't mean you have to like their behavior. With the pain you went through in your childhood – we truly are soul-mates. People used to make fun of my pimples and my nose, too. Your failed relationships and all, you are exactly the type of person I need in my life."

We hugged again, and there was a moment of silence between us as we took it all in. It was hard to believe that he had been teased just like me.

"We share a soul, Frankie Mae. You, my lady, are truly my destiny, and you have felt that for a long time now. I just want to take care of you the way a man is supposed to without all the public scrutiny and drama. You must listen to me and be ready for all the bad things the media is going to do to me. Love me and I will feel your love wherever I am, baby. As one, we will make it so that the media will never find out about us. You must promise me you will not tell anyone about this until I die. It's going to be easier getting through the hard days knowing that you love me, Frankie Mae. Do it from afar. Always keep me alive for the world, Frankie Mae. If you see me in another woman's arms, I am fulfilling a job and nothing more. The world will know that my heart is not full; because they may never get to know you, Frankie Mae. You are too special of a girl for me to feed to the beast of the media. I already know that you're gonna be alright with that. But I will always know the depth of your love by simply looking into your eyes. I will always know." Next, my man held me in his arms, sealing our love forever.

"Yes, it's true. I don't want to ever leave you, Michael. I need your love so badly. What are you talking about?"

Michael's beautiful face became sad. He placed his hands on my shoulders and scooted back into the corner of a quiet street in San Francisco. "Baby, there are going to be not only bad things, but awful things that the media is going to conjure up about me. A lot of it will be hard for you to believe. I will have to fight off the fans, fight off the media, and fight off all kinds of things that are going to shock an innocent, beautiful chocolate drop like you.

"Baby, in order to be world famous, I have to please the world. I can't simply be a man of one sex, have one love, be one color, and have one heart. My whole life will have to be divided among the masses who all love me. Having this private moment with you is so pure and so rare to me, Frankie Mae. My life is so publicly complicated that my special woman has to be either just like me, or she has to be so famous that it doesn't make a difference to the media who she is. Look, promise me something?"

"I will do anything for you, Michael Jackson. Just name it, baby," I said, cupping his cold face.

"If you never see me again, baby, uphold my name. Know in your heart I am a proud black man who loves this black woman," he declared, pointing to my heart.

At that moment as the moon faded, Michael pulled me to his chest. He kissed me with hot lips on a cold night more passionately than I had ever been kissed. He stopped – then he kissed me again until our hot kisses were sweetened by love. As Michael Jackson kissed me, a hot tear slid from his eye onto my cheek. He didn't have to tell me of his pain or how much he wanted to share me with the world; I could tell by his tears, by his touch, that he couldn't. Later, when faced with the difficult tasks before us, my own tears would be tremendous. But as we say in the ghetto, "I got this!"

"Uphold our love and marry me, Frankie Mae. Even if I am not physically there to be a part of the ceremony, you must promise me this union that will solidify our love forever. Deny the press, deny the media, deny my family – just write about our love fully when the light goes out on this shell," he begged, pointing to his chest.

"Share your love for me with the world, Frankie Mae. Tell them about this day and make sure you let my fans know that picture in the store window could have been any one of them. Tell them how we met, how I came into your life over a picture, and how, as your one and only true secret love, I cherished you. There is going to be a real reason why you can't let go of my memory. It's because you are mine and one day you will see that holding all of this love inside of you will not be enough room to contain such a love. You belong to me for eternity, and one day our true ghetto love will belong to the masses.

"Today, right here and now, it's all about you, baby. You are my one and only woman. You are my heart and soul. If you don't have the words to tell the world about our secret love, my spirit will guide the way. I will be there when I am not there to place your hands to the strokes. You need to hammer it all out and tell the world about our love. Never doubt for one minute, Frankie Mae, that I am not with you. From the day I first saw that picture of you in that vacant store window and read your novel, I have been with you. I am one hundred percent fully yours!"

As I followed his heart, everything he told me came true. I never had nor did I want to have sex with another man. My heart, mind, body, and soul belonged to only Michael Jackson. As I had stolen his heart, I was taken care of fully by my love; yet I wanted no material possessions from Michael Jackson, save his love. I rode the bus to my security job with a new car he bought me sitting in my #12 parking stall. I kept the same normalcy by taking overtime from Lita when I could to save money for my boys' college fund. I rented an old two-bedroom apartment on East 24th Street in Oakland with a broken gate and dry rot that was eating the structure to the ground. I wore old clothes and I lived on a stipend from my man that covered all of our bills, leaving a brand new car, the latest model Nissan Maxima, in the garage mainly for grocery shopping. He insisted that I save my meager wages for a rainy day. I did.

All I wanted and got from the King of Pop from the '80s until the end of his short life was his secure, untested love. Being loved by Michael Jackson meant work, but the love was the sweetest I ever had. I rode in the limousine with him until his physical dying earth date and I worried about him more than his own mother did. The media would have recognized love immediately had they seen Michael Jackson with Frankie Mae Tyson. I understood every minute of it and I knew all the details of how to be with a man with such superstardom.

Michael loved gay people. He adored the entire gay community and he had a huge following in the Bay Area that saw him with me many times and would never say a word. But Michael was 100% heterosexual. His appeal to all people, to all races, to all sexes, was as real as my love is for him today, and I will never forget the day I physically met Michael Joseph Jackson. Not for as long as I live.

In God We Trust

Several months into our relationship I did everything to resume a normal life, and at each corner something threatened to blow the lid off my secret. Michael visited my low-end apartment in East Oakland regularly, and in short order that fine man called our shack home. Often he ironed my security guard uniform for work or cooked spaghetti dinner for the boys, and he never missed making us a big pitcher of our favorite red Kool-Aid. Clad in disguises and armed with a heartfelt desire to have love he could not share with the public, Michael Jackson came with his risks.

Soon after we met, I stayed put for the Michael Jackson handlers, specifically the agent, for he had warned me he would be calling me every day with Michael's schedule. I was told to be ready for anything. I prepped for passports, wigs, disguises, and a special pass to fly on Michael's private jet. Booked from here till three months in the afterworld, Michael Jackson's handlers did their job, making sure that I wanted for nothing. I was even given a 160-page agreement to sign at a table on Michael's two-million-dollar jet. I didn't read a damn thing and was offended by the lawyers for making me sign off on promises that Michael and I had already agreed on. I signed the long forms anyway, cussing every step of the way. The only thing I ever remembered about the contract was the last line of the agreement, which asked me to tell the world about our ghetto love from my perspective in the event anything ever happened to Michael Jackson. Michael even gave me the name of the book he wanted me to write. He called it *The Love He Saved*, based on one of his early hits with the Jackson 5.

It was not going to be a book I'd write, because I wanted him to outlive me. In the contract he said that telling the world of our ghetto love gave credence to an important part of his superstardom existence that he could not publicly disclose. He wanted this book to honor his fans and to let them know that any one of them could have been me, Frankie Mae. Michael's generosity to his fans could never be matched by another superstar. I was overcome with pride signing this long piece of paper.

I read further and discovered that I was to come out with the details of our relationship within one year of his passing. I stopped reading for a moment and watched the lawyers talk to Michael on their cell phones. Tears streamed down my face. It was the first time I had even thought about living on this planet without Michael Jackson. When your lover is already the best in the world, there is no replacement for his affections. I dried my tears and completed the paperwork, thinking that in honor of his sometimes secretive Muslim faith, I owed this man my life.

I had always been candid with my man, cussing, acting a fool, and throwing a fit or two here and there, thinking at first Michael would be so through with me, but he liked all that ghetto mess. During countless trips, I was dropped off in places not knowing where the handlers were taking me. By now we had seen the world together. At each stop, Michael was there in all his glory to meet me, for if I was not going to live like a queen, he'd bring all this stuff to me. As he promised when we met, Michael did not judge me in honoring the pact we made on our fateful meeting day. He respected me as an equal soul-mate and he never, ever tried to make me into something that I was not. He read everything I wrote, begging me to find a "real" publisher. He hated not giving me the worldly things that would make my life more comfortable. Yet he understood I needed his love, not material support. My independence literally ate him apart, until he really got to know that my happiest moments in life were truly the ones that I spent in his arms or simply in his company. Following his infinite wisdom, I pray for the day to resume our eternal love and live in a place where there will be no need to sign off on love through attorneys.

Michael Jackson, 1983

Two years into our relationship, *Thriller* was a killer on record charts. The album stayed at the top of the charts for over 36 weeks. "Billie Jean" swept the states and was a hit overseas, including the UK. "Beat it," "Wanna Be Startin' Somethin'," and "Thriller" all hit top ten. On March 25, 1983, I received red roses every hour of the day as my sons and I prepared to watch Michael Jackson perform on Motown 25. I had ridden all day on the bus, waiting for the call. Earlier in the day, Michael almost gave my boss Lita and my co-workers a heart attack.

Once a month, a guard was chosen to receive the "Employee of the Month" award. In February 1983 I was a happy woman. My man was doing well at the top, and I was doing well at the bottom. When I told Michael about the award, he insisted on being at the department store a day before Motown 25 hit the air. At first I thought his request was an impossible request that could not be pulled off. Now, I'd have to tell Lita something to arrange a way for Michael to be at this stupid-ass ceremony. This went against all of our plans. I won the argument, and Michael agreed he'd watch the awards ceremony from my surveillance area. We prayed that in Oakland, California, nobody would find out Michael Jackson was hiding in the surveillance room to see his baby get a security guard award.

Only Lita, the janitor, and I had a key to the room. Michael would hide in the room and peep into the gold keyhole ceremony to watch me receive the award, and all other ways of his being there were out of the question.

On his way to Oakland two hours before the ceremony, we argued on the phone as I tried to stop him from coming. To me this shit of Michael hiding in a small closet was silly as hell. During the call one of his many doubles had taken an assignment to fill in as Michael in varying world locations. The man in the background even sounded just like Michael. I was stunned that Michael would use doubles to fill in for him while he supported my getting a security guard award

"I told you not to do this over some silly-ass award," I complained. "This is not what our relationship is all about, Michael, and you know that. I love it that nobody knows we're together." Michael hated it when I questioned his decisions. Always in control of his schedule – nothing was going to stop Michael Jackson from being there for me on my special day.

"Why, I am doing this for you, baby. Don't be silly, Frankie Mae. You know how much I love you and how much it hurts me to be away from you. *Thriller* has been such a success and I don't care about that right now. Everybody wants a piece of me. I hire doubles all the time to be me. You know that, and we both know that album will go down in history and my missing one day of touring will not kill sales. I have to please all the fans, Frankie Mae. Now, I want to be in that room when you receive that work award. Those kinds of things are about family. You are my family and your life is very important to me," he cried.

I listened, holding the telephone to my ear, feeling like the luckiest woman in the world. I couldn't wait for what he was going to say next.

"They want pictures with me, they want interviews, everything. I can't be in all these places at once. I can't believe you wouldn't allow me this special day to see you get your award." I listened to the pain in my man's voice, knowing I could not deny him this moment.

"You always complain about my job, Michael."

"Because you're doing something that you don't have to do, Frankie Mae. How many times do I have to tell you, I can . . . ?"

I cut him off. We'd had this conversation before, with him forgetting our greatest moments were a tribute to our discretionary secret. Of all the places to hide in the world, being public in the ghetto was the most secret place for anyone famous to hide. I was not going to ruin his feelings for me, nor mine for him by coming out with our relationship and changing my kids' and my comfortable life.

"Michael?"

"Yes, baby."

"I love you too much to keep reminding you why our relationship has survived the media glare."

"Frankie Mae, all you have to do is leave that little room door open for me so I can see your honor. The agent will get me an unmarked car. I will call my double to fill in for *Thriller* publicity, okay?" He waited. "Come on, I can't do anything until you say yes," he moaned.

"Thanks, Michael," I said, taking a deep breath. "Call me back with the details. It will mean the world to me for you to be there," I stated lovingly.

On the day of the event, as soon as Lita entered the auditorium to set up for the awards ceremony, a raggedy '73 Mustang entered my security station for check-in. I wrote down the license plate number, guiding the driver to the visitor parking. Next, an old woman dressed like Tyler Perry's Madea took my surveillance key. The old woman smiled at me and then kissed me on the right cheek on her way to my surveillance station.

Michael had no problem hiding in that surveillance room to watch me receive the security guard award. At least fifty people walked past the old lady, never knowing it was Michael Jackson. I was laughing like a madwoman as I received my award. It felt good knowing that the world's greatest entertainer was doing all of this just to be with me, and that was the real honor of this day.

It was actions like these on his part that showed me he really loved me. I know that if I had been a stranger on the street, Michael Jackson would have bent over backwards to give me a moment of glory in the sun, for the sacrifice on Michael's part never stopped with the family he so loved.

He wanted to put the kids and me in a mansion even more after this event. Again, I appreciated the life we lived already. He had already picked us out a maid and a home. I said no, no, and no. He even threatened to end our relationship over these rejections. I kept saying no. Later, Michael took my "Employee of the Month" award home to his mansion. Now whenever I visit the mansion, I can see the award posted prominently in the middle of all his silver, gold, platinum, and multi-platinum records, videos, and Grammy awards.

"Michael, I don't want to get into this with you again," I yelled into the phone. "I ain't trying to be on top of your success. The way the media and your fans treat you, baby, is too scary for me to put my kids or myself through, and if your fame continues to grow, the white man ain't gonna have it, and all of this is gonna kill you," I shouted. He'd heard this argument a million times.

"I don't judge people by color, Frankie Mae. But part of loving a person is sharing what you have with them. Sharing everything you have with that person is a perfectly normal thing to do. Agree?"

"I'm sorry, baby. The media is famous for breaking stars down. No. I don't agree with that," I shot back, honoring his need for me to stay me.

"I can't believe that you and the kids are happy living like that in Oakland."

"Living like what, Michael? Is there something wrong with this life?" I shouted. "You keep the roof over our heads. You do everything for us just fine and you're always there for special life events. Now here you are wanting to do everything for us, yet you're not appreciating the happiness that you have given us in simply hiding our relationship. You give me more when I am happy with you already. I am happy with what I got and I just don't know when you will ever believe that, and it's starting to bother me."

"That's why I love you so much, Frankie Mae. You're so unbelievable," he chimed lovingly.

"We love you, Michael Jackson. All I want you to

do is go out there and give them that backwards slide move that you have been showing the kids and blow the world away."

"For real?" he asked, childlike.

"For real," I answered back. Just hours ago, the world's biggest entertainer had hidden out in a broom closet to watch his baby receive an innocuous award. Today, Michael Jackson was going to shock Planet Earth with a dance called "The Moonwalk."

"Here we go. It's so hard, even after two years, to say goodbye to you. You will always be the lady of my life."

"Is that another song, Michael?"

"I wrote it the day I met you, Frankie Mae. I still can't believe that your dad used to talk to Joseph."

"Michael, they were good friends in Gary. He used to tell my father he wanted to be a blues star. Daddy told Mother he said if he didn't make it, his kids would. Now look," I said happily. "Love you."

"Girl, had I seen you then . . ."

"You'd a been too young." I laughed.

"You'd have waited."

"Right," I answered. "Love you."

"I love you more," he argued. Michael hung up the telephone this night not believing how close we'd been to each other when we were children and regretting that no matter what he did, Frankie was going to be Frankie no matter what. I was high enough off his love to giggle as he laughed at me, telling me he was sickened by how much I loved him. Even though it was just minutes before the show, he kept this up.

"You at least accept the flowers and kisses I send you, right?" he asked.

"Of course I do," I answered back.

"Kids okay?"

"I already told you so, silly. You know they're fine, Michael. I am glad you agreed to go on and do the Motown Twenty-five anniversary show. Break a leg before you miss your destiny," I said, using an old show business term.

"You just wait until you see what I am going to do with these legs tonight." He laughed. Next he told me about the black and silver outfit he was wearing, down to the beaded socks and black penny loafers. And then he asked me if it was all right for him to give Diana Ross a kiss. I hated the bitch but I told him yes. I said as long as it was not Dame Elizabeth Taylor, I didn't care who he kissed. Tonight if he didn't get off the phone, he'd miss his turn. I knew at that very moment Michael Jackson was going to glide into superstardom after this show. He had been calling me for weeks about his new moonwalk and had even practiced it with the kids, who were ecstatic. He had described it to the kids again over the phone tonight, and his agent had to snatch the phone out of his hands to get him ready for the stage.

Minutes after the first call of the night, Michael escaped his agent to say he wanted our love to stay so pure that nothing would get in the way of my anonymity. He said this knowing that after tonight at the Motown 25 reunion, it would be hard for us to catch special moments like we had together again. Michael had a great sense of humor. He said he was going to surprise the world tonight. So he sent the kids and me a beautiful new television set so that we could watch the event that would change the world in full living color. The kids read his letters over and over, promising never to mention our secret outside of the house. They never did.

Now the kids and I were wearing sequined gloves, putting them on as soon as we heard the opening beat to "Billie Jean." Since Michael came into our lives, the kids were healthier and happier than they'd been before. I met and fell in love with Michael Jackson, and the feeling was unreal. Though we kept our life simple, they wanted for nothing regarding health care, food, and regular school needs. They loved Michael more than anything and they relished each and every moment they spent with the superstar they called Dad.

Later, wearing a distinctive sequined glove, Michael snapped his head to the right. He looked dead into the audience. Afterwards he did his moonwalk so well I didn't catch the rest of the show because I had passed out on the floor during the TV crowd's standing ovation. By the time I came to, the kids, dressed in their red and black Thriller jackets, were in the kitchen doing the moonwalk like their father. After the performance, Michael called.

"Baby, what did you think about it?" he asked. I was so proud of Michael Jackson I could not talk at first. The kids screamed happily into the phone; this was the proudest moment of our lives.

"She fainted, Daddy!" Shuun screamed, scaring Michael.

Later, I talked to my man about how great he was with the kids as they were still screaming over my shoulder. Michael said he loved all of us and he told me to go to bed and wait for him. Tonight he kept saying he loved me like I was the only thing he cared about in the world. The kids chimed into the phone that we were already together. Michael agreed. I thanked him for the Disneyland tickets, for being at my awards ceremony the day before, and for everything. I thanked him for the keys to a new Nissan Maxima and for making my life easier. I thanked him for the kind words that he delivered to the children daily. We cried because we both knew that after tonight, it would be even harder for us to ever be alone with the superstar Michael Jackson again.

"Baby, your life is going to change even more, if you can believe it," I told him.

"Don't say that, Frankie Mae. I am doing all of this so that one day you, me, and our kids will be together forever."

It was hard to guard the department store with a huge smile on my face that contradicted my life. Guys hit on me all the time at work. I turned them all down. Lita introduced me to her brother, Ted, saying it was time for me to get a daddy for them kids, without knowing I had the best daddy they could ever need. Ted thought I was the perfect catch until I told him and Lita I had somebody already. When Lita asked who, I never said another word.

I knew that it would be very hard to preserve our love. After Motown 25, I talked to Michael on the telephone less. Even our trips to the mansion became less and less. His world fame had grown larger in, out, and around the entire world. As the demand for Michael's attention went up, there were not enough impersonators in the world to fill Michael's shoes. My love soared, I was so proud, but I saw him much less.

On February 28, 1984, Michael went to the Grammys with Brooke Shields and Webster, not knowing that my pain of seeing him with her sent me to a Highland Hospital emergency room with chest pains.

With all of the hoopla about the awards, I finished my shift at work with an ambulance ride to the emergency room. Michael was holding Webster on one side, and Brooke Shields on the other, wearing a beautiful drop pearl necklace with a black and white one-shoulder gown and black shoes. The picture of them together literally almost killed me. I had to deal with it alone. He had called me just minutes before the cameras began to roll on the red carpet to tell me he was going to wear the royal blue and gold studded jacket I had picked out for him a few days ago. Knowing me, he said that he and Brooke Shields were not interested in each other sexually. He'd known her since he was thirteen and promised me that no sparks had ever jumped off between them.

During this conversation I could hear Brooke Shields laughing in the background about how many awards Michael was going to win for *Thriller*. I was jealous and wanted to cuss the bitch out later as I watched Michael thank Epic Records, Jackie Wilson, and other greats in the music business. I remembered how Michael had prepared me for such a day, knowing one day that my simple attitude about his success could change. The chatter in the background was of fans who wanted Michael's autograph as if nobody else was around him.

While Michael Jackson's life took off, my love for him became more secret than ever before. At work I guarded the facility, never telling coworkers of a specific love life. I stayed away from my family in Los Angeles to hide my love for Michael Jackson. Sometimes I could not believe our relationship was real. No one with an ounce of sense would believe the pain and the love I was experiencing. Still, Michael called me daily to make sure that I was going to stay in his camp. His life was already in the stratosphere, so where was I going to go? I did not want anything or anyone to spoil the strong love that Michael and I shared that apparently he could never find in another woman. On this night while the world and movie stars celebrated Michael Jackson, I was signing the next of kin on my emergency medical card with a big fat zero.

Memories

"All the years that we have been doing this . . ." Michael Jackson said over the telephone. He kept talking, as I didn't have to ask him a thing. Together we had succeeded in many ways in our most secret love relationship. We survived many of my jealous rages by Michael reporting to the news media that he was asexual. We had evaded the news, fooled the fans – even his own family. Our relationship was secret in every sense of the word, and I paid for it in ways you'd never imagine.

Each time I heard bad press about Michael, I spent the day throwing up or crying. It was hard to pull it off sometimes, but we did it because Michael was so good at keeping me special in his life. I was so average looking and still so ghetto that guards, or some of Michael's own handlers, would toss me out of places, never having a clue about what I meant to the King of Pop. Stuff like this hurt Michael, for he could not always be there to cover up the details. Those were the only times when he'd have to confront handlers, literally telling them to take their hands off me without explaining why.

The hard times were really hard, and a few years into our relationship, I thought each day that I'd get the call that Michael was calling it off with me. Seeing him go through his pain publicly hurt my children. I spent hours explaining the lies to them. These lies hurt the kids more than it did anyone because they knew their dad was not capable of doing the bad things to kids that we heard on the news.

Worst of all for me was going through the Pepsi tragedy together, but apart. Afterwards, I made each trial date Michael had without one person ever recognizing me. I had disguises designed especially for my kids, Michael, and me. We studied old costume geniuses like artist Robert Edmond Jones. Michael hired designers with the cadence to possess strong visual deception capabilities as well as a thorough knowledge of illusionary draping. We spent months finding, creating materials, and getting fitted and drafted for textiles and costumes. Our need for ongoing human deception was great.

The costume designer was serious and effective in creating human drapery that leant complete mystique to hiding the frames of three of the most important players in Michael Jackson's life. He was the same inspiration for the red drapes you often saw over the faces of Prince and Paris and even little Blanket, before we knew them so well.

For over twenty-eight years, to friends, family, and others, I was a single parent of two boys struggling to get by as a security guard in a floundering Oakland department store. To Michael Jackson, I was Frankie Mae, his ever-loving ghetto rat. I was the woman he loved, the woman who kept all of his secrets, the woman who wanted nothing from him but love. I believed in Michael Jackson 100%. Suffice it to say, my love never wavered.

Over the years of hiding, I always wanted to face women like Lisa Marie Presley, Debbie Rowe, and Brooke Shields for having the public attention of my Michael. He never loved any of these women, and I flat out detested Dame Elizabeth Taylor. Debbie Rowe was so plain, ugly, and money hungry that I never gave the woman a second thought. When those feelings occurred, Michael always stepped in to soothe and justify his need to have a public persona that would appease his many adoring fans.

"Frankie, I don't ever want to hear you say you hate anyone," he once said to me. Had Michael actually introduced me to the world, who would suspect that I, a high school dropout with fucked-up teeth, could be anything to Michael Jackson? I was the perfect ruse for his love peace, the perfect deception for him. For (according to him) he needed someone, and that person was always me.

Invisible

During Michael's peak years in the '80s, the world contemplated Michael Jackson's sexuality, and at the same time he became the best lover in the world to me. With all that Michael ignited in me sexually, I was the one laughing at the media who could not figure out that this fine, chocolate entertainer was a man. He knew how to kiss a woman passionately and he knew how to bring a woman to one climax after another. Time is short in the entertainment business. To us, the less they knew the better.

With secrets came a great deal of pain. That pain was worth going through to be with Michael Jackson. He knew my pert, firm breasts, he knew my curves, my lips, my pain, and my emotions. He knew and appreciated all these things about me as I knew all these wonderful things about him.

But thankfully to the world we were invisible. Our union was the most successful secret the media world would never know, and for that I had the very best of Michael Jackson. Those albums had nothing next to the performances I saw Michael Jackson put out in bed. Hell, those fancy moves had to come from somewhere. You figure out the rest. Michael and I were determined to save our love. As hard as all of this was, by June 25, 2009, I would be proud that ours was the love Michael Jackson kept to his heart. I was devastated each day that he was gone. I had always hoped he'd take this special love to his death, and one day he would.

I Remember When

Whenever Michael came to Oakland, California, he stayed up all night. I knew my man, and his being awake was as familiar to me as his ever-changing, beautiful face. His voice always sounded tired. There would be times he lay next to me all night, never sleeping. I fell asleep as soon as my head met his chest or as soon as we finished making love. My clit would be shaking for hours after feeling his nice, hard manhood inside of me. I'd wake up sometimes seeing him in my security guard uniform.

"What are you doing up, baby?" I asked, sitting up straight in our black lacquer bed that was designed to be a '67 Ford Mustang.

"You know I can't sleep, Frankie Mae. This uniform would look good on stage," he joked. Mine was a simple light- and dark-blue uniform made out of cheap polyester. The badge, #233, was cheaper and looked like something you'd find at a toy store. Michael could make me laugh about anything, but he was looking cute and serious about this uniform. He stood in front of the gold-trimmed mirrored closet door, touching my silver badge and saluting to me like a real soldier. I laughed, too, because it was funny seeing Michael standing in front of a closet door that had been sliding off the roller for two years. The door was so crooked I hollered. The chipped glass above Michael's head would have been too much even for the tabloids. Nobody would believe that Michael Jackson would be caught dead in my ghetto shack.

"You don't have to do this. I can read your mind," he reminded me, taking off the uniform and then hanging it back up on the brown wire hanger. I gave him the "you ought to quit" look.

Michael looked beautiful later when he climbed into the bed next to me. He wanted the kids and me to have the mansion in Beverly Hills. He talked about cars, money, and all that came with fame. However, I was a simple ghetto rat, and he had lost me. Having his love was something I wanted for the rest of my life; I couldn't give a damn about Michael's money. Going so public with houses, cars, and other possessions would ruin what we had in a day. The media would drag my marriages, my kids, and all the indiscretions of my youth through the mud – even the fact that I dropped out of school for fear of getting beat up over a Michael Jackson song. The fine bitches would frown and say, "What the fuck he want with that sorry bitch?" The ugly chicks would smile and say it could have been them. Then they'd become groupies, using each and every opportunity to steal my man away from me.

The media would do to me what they did to that other ugly bitch Susan Boyle. They heard her sing one cool note, and they launched her into superstardom in Great Britain overnight. Next thing I knew, they were calling that bitch an ugly retard that needed a makeover; now her album is number one.

And that's not to speak of my job at the department store as a rent-a-cop. Oh, hell no. The media would eat my ass alive.

"You know what we agreed on, baby," I reminded him in a soft voice.

He then heard one of his old tunes on my fuzzy radio. He launched his entire body over mine to turn up the right knob on the old radio. "Did you like 'Off the Wall'?" he asked.

I rolled over, letting the cover expose my big, luscious, sweet ghetto butt. "I liked the album cover. You had more hair then," I joked.

Michael put his hand on my butt. Then he kissed my inner thighs, working his way into wet chartered territory. He turned the music down so we could get it on. I protested.

"Turn it up, Michael," I moaned. "You know I like that one," I said excitedly. Michael turned it up alright. I closed my eyes. Soon the kids heard the song. With that, I jumped into my pajamas quickly with Michael helping me pull up my yellow pants. We both laughed before they made it to my room. When they arrived, we acted innocent, while Shuun was the loudest about hearing Daddy on the radio.

"Living off the wall . . ." he started singing. The baby giggled loudly.

"I am going to have to put you both in a video, little Shuun," Michael said happily. "You can really sing!"

"Serious?" Shuun asked. They were all on the bed with us now. Michael looked at me, knowing what to say to Shuun (seven) and Daryle (two).

"Buddy, I wish I could . . . but your mother over there will not have it," he said to Shuun in a soft, caring voice.

"I love you, Daddy," Shuun said to him, hugging his neck. Then Daryle grabbed the other side of Michael's neck while he held his diaper up with the other. The baby accidentally knocked the old radio we had on the nightstand to the floor, killing Michael's song. He said, "I love you," to him, too.

"I love you both more!" Michael said back excitedly. Michael tried to fix the radio, and we all laughed when Michael Jackson looked at us all pitifully. I covered his mouth before he offered to buy us this and that. I didn't want to hear it, when the most important thing I needed from him was love. Then he handed me the broken radio as he bounced off the bed to tend to my kids.

"Who wants Kool-Aid?" Michael asked. To the screams of "I do" from all of us, Michael raced to the kitchen to make us some red Kool-Aid. Later, I heard him playing with the kids, who simply adored Michael. He then changed baby Daryle's dirty diaper and put them back to bed.

Next, he came back to my room with a red dollar-store tumbler, dripping on the sides with Kool-Aid and large chunks of jagged ice. He had even placed a slice of an old dry lemon on the side of the tumbler just for me.

He got under the covers with me like a child, telling me I had done a great job raising Shuun and Daryle. His kind words made me smile. He loved kids. To me, his care for children was uncontestable.

Tonight he also loved my feet. He said it was hot in the house. He leaped out of bed again to go turn on the air conditioning. Soon he was back, looking at my toenails that were kind of chipped. I didn't like pedicures like most girls do. My job as a guard required I wear comfortable black sneakers. To me it was a waste of money to pamper myself. I was natural from top to bottom and didn't really have the time to be doing something with feet nobody would ever see. In simple terms, I was a little ghetto and loving it. So long as Michael was happy, Brooke Shields and Webster were at home, the kids were happy, and my job didn't fire me for having jacked feet, life was good for me.

Rank feet or not, Michael had a way of playing This Little Piggy with my feet. He liked taking my toes apart one by one. He kissed each toe carefully, to my complete arousal.

"These old corns have walked a million miles," he joked, kissing them tenderly.

"Stop it!" I laughed, pulling my foot away from him playfully.

"Stop what?" he asked kiddingly, putting my toes back into his mouth.

"Stop tickling me," I'd cry, feeling so loved. On this special night, early in our long relationship, we stopped for a moment to study one another's eyes, as the room filled up with cool, fresh air. A fresh ring of red Kool-Aid left a mustache on his now light skin. With jazz playing in the background of a quiet, serene night, I touched his face gently, loving every minute of him. We both closed our eyes and held each other tightly. He grabbed my hairbrush off the dresser to accept his award.

"I'd like to thank Epic Records for this great love and these wonderful two boys who have been a great influence in my life," he announced. I lay in the bed feeling safer with him here, away from the red carpet and all of those movie stars. Loving how it happened and yet determined to keep this love simple, normal, and tucked as far away from the world as we possibly could. I brought my knees up to my chin and laughed.

Following a long embrace, sweat dribbled down the sides of our faces in anticipation of the great sex we relished. My pussy was super wet. My torn-up toes were dancing, while his manhood got harder by the second. There was serious foreplay as I took my turn kissing, licking, and sucking each and every crevice of Michael Jackson's body. It was so good I moaned. Then he moaned. When he came in my mouth, it tasted better than a white milkshake; I longed for more and more.

From that moment on, we spent an hour holding each other, building up numerous times to what was perfect sexual pleasure. Later, we made wild, passionate love again and again all through the night. Michael was a generous and considerate lover who took his time exploring my body, getting me ready from every angle for more. Michael always saved the best of his love for me.

Each time we made love, I reached the most enormous climaxes ever. I needed him. His being so distant all the time only enhanced my need to love him. Through all the challenges this great entertainer would endure in his life, I had never, ever let Michael Jackson down.

Carrying the Torch for Michael Jackson

As I sit here in my lone apartment looking back on my love for Michael Jackson, it surprises me how much I loved him and how far I went to protect that love. I was there for my man at every turn. He and I raised my children and just tried to preserve a part of the life we had together that no one would ever infringe upon.

Protecting love meant keeping secrets. Keeping a low profile for so long was very hard, as I endured all his pain as his lover. At work people were curious of my love life, but I hid everything. I hid the love, the kids, the gifts, the cars, and my feelings for the only man in the world I loved. At work I did what I was told quicker than anyone so that the spotlight would not end up shining on me. I stayed out of mansions, clubs, bars, and events that would foster the rumors, and when the kids and I visited the mansion, we traveled in unmarked tinted cars and jets, always wearing our disguises. However, one day on my way to work, just about two years after I met Michael, I remembered what Michael had told me about the paparazzi.

It was a Monday following a secret outing with Michael and the kids, when a paparazzo jumped out of the bushes for an interview. I had been with Michael for years, and nothing like this had ever happened before. For anyone to know about me was a stretch. I had parked the car in my usual garden spot where I had been parking it for years. Dressed in my usual blue polyester uniform with my hair braided down to my waist, I was the lone person on the fourth floor of the floundering store's parking garage. The man with the huge camera over his shoulder was a huge white guy with red hair and blue eyes. Carrying a huge lens, he shucked the bag off and around his shoulders. As the black leather case was abandoned to the ground, the man ran up to me. He stuck the camera in my face.

"How does it feel being the secret lover of the King of Pop?" he asked. I placed the strap of my purse over my right shoulder, picking up the pace. Unlike other victims of the press, I had nothing to say to this man. I grew up on the wild side. He caught me on a good day, a day when I didn't feel like cussing him out. Michael laughed when I threw certain looks his way or acted ghetto. Husband number two had left me after one of my ghetto acts. It was an act Michael had seen twice, but it was an act that truly could knock an unsuspecting intruder off guard. But my man knew what those looks meant, and he loved me for me. I was a little woman – but I could get down if I had to. While this fool followed me, I took in deep breaths, trying to keep him at bay.

"Oh, so it's like that. You're one of those chicks not looking for fame. Have to respect that," he said. Next the man removed the lens cover. He picked up his case and then he backed away without shooting the flash. That was the only time the paparazzi had ever approached me.

"Well," Lita chimed in later. "Tell me now, why would the press be following little ol' you, Frankie Mae?" she asked as she watched the paparazzo haul into a white van and leave the parking lot. "Could it be the rumors are true?" She reached in the tin slot to hand me my time card.

"Thanks," I said, taking the card. "What rumors you talkin' bout, Lita?"

"Word is out that you're sleeping with Michael Jackson," she stated.

"Girl, if you believe that, I got some bridges I want to sell you," I shot back. She came back quicker.

"You ain't gonna be able to hide something like this forever, Frankie Mae. All the paparazzi ain't as nice as that one was," she advised.

I had to ignore her. "What shift I got Saturday, Lita?"

"What shift you want, Ms. Michael Jackson?" she asked. A little of the ghetto got out as I pulled Lita over to the side of the counter and up to my chest. I had to get real with her ass now. If anybody heard something like this, it could ruin my relationship with Michael permanently.

"Look, Lita," I started.

She pushed me hard into the broom closet behind the lone desk I had worked at for years. "I wouldn't go there if I was you, Frankie Mae," she warned.

Feeling more defensive, I tightened my grip on my boss. "Ain't any use in you trying to hang all up in my grill, or my personal life, Lita. Sometimes things just happens in a person's life you have to leave alone. I am a single parent just trying to raise my kids like everybody else. I get it on here and there, but it ain't anybody's business who I am fucking. Be real with your shit, Lita, and I will be real with mine. Have you taken a look at me lately? You know I got two baby daddies and ain't ne'er one been around for years," I said, dropping her in my chair.

"I understand what you trying to do—"

I cut Lita off with tears pouring out of my eyes. "If you really understand, then don't ask me questions like this anymore. I still can't afford to get my damn teeth fixed right. What would a rap star want with this, Lita?" I asked her, pointing to myself. My boss checked me out real close, knowing I was lying about my long relationship with Michael. Feeling it was better to join my lie, she agreed to leave this alone, confirming my schedule for the upcoming Saturday. Lita walked out of the lobby, leaving me sorry I had to deal with her that way.

~~~

The fight we had earlier was so serious that later in the day, word was out never to ask Frankie Mae who she was dating. And stop the Michael Jackson rumors. She must be dating an impersonator, because who in their right damn mind would want her ghetto ass? "The girl is very defensive about her personal life and she goes off at the drop of a dime," Lita offered. After hearing it going down like that with Lita and my job, I knew my secret was still safe.

It was hard defending my secret lifestyle, but it was hell worth it to me. I had three people to protect, and with that came a lifestyle that was simple for me and the boys. I put extra money away for their college dreams. Michael preserved our simple lifestyle through accountants who paid all the $800-a-month rent for twenty years in advance. Michael sent me a black MasterCard every day for two years, until one day I finally started using it. I used it for food and clothing, nothing extravagant that would place a spotlight on our love.

Before I went to bed this night, my love called me
~~~

simply to say he loved me and to kiss the boys good night. I had to tell him about what happened with old nosy-ass Lita. I even threw in what they said about me and the Michael impersonator I was fucking, and he laughed so hard. The paparazzi were like snakes, he said. He complimented me for handling the guy and Lita the way I had.

This personal side of Michael Jackson was so pure, so real, and so normal that the world would never be entitled to know about it. They'd never ruin this love, for it was so well protected; and more importantly, this love was mine and I took it seriously.

Sleepless Nights

Oftentimes, when I woke to go to work, Michael would simply lie right next to me nursing a new cup of Kool-Aid with his eyes wide open. His inability to sleep was real, and it bothered me. But Michael's life was so full of things to be bothered by, I simply tried to make his life as real and comfortable as I could while he was with me.

This night, as he said the usual things to me in his sweet, soft voice, I had learned never to question Michael Jackson's insomnia. He never took drugs in my presence. He held meetings with the children often, warning them, "Never use drugs."

He spent loads of time playing with my kids, who loved him unconditionally. When Michael did sleep, he always looked peaceful. I could tell by observing him over the years that sleep was the most difficult thing for Michael Jackson to come by. Most of the time he was with me he was awake or he was in my boys' room telling them beautiful bedtime stories. Or he was on the telephone talking to the people who handled his very busy life. My job was an easy job to do, for I had become very good at simply being me and being his close confidante. Many of Michael's handlers went bye-bye over my advice to Michael. I never changed a thing about myself, my job, my kids, or my life, for I had to be there for Michael Jackson in the real way he needed.

In one conversation I had with him before his passing, our long relationship had taken a significant turn. Michael seemed to be distant and more forlorn, and it worried me.

"Michael. The kids are grown now. You have your beautiful three children, and it's time to look deeper into this sleep problem you've had for years," I confided.

"What have I told you about that, Frankie Mae?" he reminded me.

I lay on the bed we had recently made love in and remained quiet for a moment. "Honey, you've had this sleeping problem for years. That 2005 trial, taking that police photo and all just made this sleeping problem worse in my opinion," I offered.

"I wish everybody understood me like you, Frankie Mae. Baby, I have to go rehearse. I don't want to talk about this right now. Is that okay with you?" he asked. Since I had met him, Michael Jackson was always very considerate of my feelings. Following so many years into our relationship and just two days before his death, my opinion was still important to him. I hugged the telephone and listened to him.

"I am going to rehearse in that beautiful red shirt you bought me when I announced the concert," he promised.

"Try and do it on your own, Michael, before asking Murray for help," I advised, referring to his expensive AEG doctor.

"Your words are always my first and last consideration, baby," he said. It was hard to believe that after all these years, Michael Jackson and I still had a problem saying goodbye to one another. Truthfully, Michael had told me that AEG paid this Doctor Murray $100,000 a month to care for him. However, I was seeing the opposite. I was seeing neglect. At this time I knew Michael J. Jackson better than anyone did. He was his own man. Nobody could push him to do a damn thing unless he wanted to. The best way to get results out of my man was to make a statement and hope it was valid enough for Michael to embrace independently. My experience proved to me that was not an easy thing to do all the time.

"I love you, MJ," I chimed.

"I love you more . . ." he said back.

In love, in secrets, my secret lover of many years was successful. In just a few hours the world reported my superstar lover's death. Just so there is no confusion, when I say "Michael Jackson," be assured it's the same Michael Joseph Jackson that we know as the "King of Pop."

Sorry about those who will be put off by this, but my union to Michael Jackson is as real to me at this very moment of his earthly passing as it was the day we both planned it. Yes, today I have the memories of the day I first fell in love with the notorious King of Pop, and now that our love will not infringe on Michael's security anymore or his safety or his hefty schedule or the many other loves who left an indelible stamp on his life – I thank you for letting me share this secret love story with you intricately and personally.

Michael Jackson, 1984

Early in January 1984, Michael and other members of the Jacksons filmed a Pepsi-Cola commercial, overseen by executive Philip Dusenberry at the Shrine Auditorium in Los Angeles. On this rare occasion, Michael surprised me one day when I came home. I had not seen him but twice since Motown. On this night he lay in the bed just waiting for me. I was glad to see my man waiting for me in bed when I got home from work. He argued, telling me to quit that damn job for God knows how many times. I argued back no as I usually did. End of the conversation.

The kids had surrounded their father with kisses and Kentucky Fried Chicken, which he loved. Afterwards, the boys locked themselves in their bedroom to figure out the new games Michael had brought home. Later, Michael and I had incredible sex. My pussy was tight like he liked it. I loved saving myself for only him. His skin had gotten lighter. His nose was smaller and he still had problems going to sleep, but he was the same man I had come to know and love over the years, no doubt.

We made passionate love six times that night. I teased him about everything from his perfectly straight hair to his obvious weight loss and his tinier nose. My man could not get enough of me, nor I him. He said he came to see me just for some sweet kisses and to catch up with this Michael Jackson impersonator who was stealing his love. The laughter we shared as a couple was unique. No two people on the planet loved the way we did. He had longed so much for my kisses that he began biting my skin. From there he never stopped kissing me the whole time he was here. He wanted to feel my skin, see me, feel me, love me.

The Price of Fame

The kids and I were very careful to take trips to see Michael. I usually planned these trips carefully around my job vacation times, which fortunately allowed me the flexibility to be free for my man. The more our romance grew, the more Michael needed my time. I had built up such a good relationship with Lita that she let me go whenever Michael needed me, keeping her promise to maintain my secret for well over twenty years.

In the '80s Michael often sent a car or a plane for the kids and me. It was during this time that Michael invited the kids and me to go backstage to see him film the Pepsi-Cola commercial. In full costume regalia, nobody recognized I was there with my kids to see Michael. Whenever anybody got too close, I acted so ghetto they backed off immediately. Today, Michael snatched off my old lady wig. He hugged the kids before asking the agent to take them backstage for some ice cream.

He held me ever so tightly, telling me he was nervous about making the commercial. I could look into his beautiful eyes and see how stressed out he was. To get away from the handlers, Michael and I got creative. One of our favorite places to hide was the bathroom. He'd let me sit on the toilet in the small room. Often he'd look down on me and tell me his happiness, his worries, and his pain. We never got busy in those stalls.

We simply grabbed what moments we could together to discuss the subject of the day. Today Michael told me he didn't like the way Pepsi had set up the pyrotechnics.

"It just doesn't look like they took the time to do anything right," he complained. I grabbed him by the waist and comforted him with a hug from my sitting position. Even as a close confidante, I respected Michael's talent, so I never elaborated on topics where I didn't have enough information. I trusted what he said and simply told my man to be careful and that I supported him. I didn't trust white folks for one minute. I had been suspicious about how they always fed the media bad things about Michael.

"Baby, the only thing you and your brothers can do is go out there and give a good performance," I told him. "Since you are so worried about this shaky setup, just be careful and have those stage men check things again. If I were you, baby, I'd watch my back."

Tears welled in his eyes. He looked exhausted as he stroked my face. We kissed passionately, trading all our worries, love, and care in our silent commitment to one another.

"I'm glad you're here," he said softly.

"I'm glad I could come," I said back.

Later, I watched him hand the kids music, gifts, and magic memorabilia as he cleaned them up after their ice cream treat. Michael always took such great care of us. His love was pure and beautiful the way he always protected us.

"I tried to keep the promise to have you guys be here with me, but the dates, the schedule, the media props – it's so hard to keep up with everything all the time," he stammered.

I was well aware of what it took to be the world entertainer he was. Our agent was superb at hiding our relationship from the media. Nobody would ever know that such a homely woman with two kids was the love of Michael's life, because it would be the only thing Michael Jackson ever had that the media and the press would never get a hold of. And if they did notice, they recognized immediately how hard we were trying to keep this love out of the spotlight.

Being apart from Michael was worth every bit of what I went through to hide the love he needed. Our love was a small morsel of life he couldn't get anywhere else in the world.

Then in front of a full house of fans during a simulated concert practice, my man's worst fears that he had discussed only moments ago came true. When it happened, I fainted. The pyrotechnics accidentally set my man's hair on fire. He had been right to tell me that the setup was not correct. To protect Michael in anticipation of the coming swarm of media, our longtime agent pulled me aside to warn me. I had been standing backstage waiting for Michael to take his break, this time disguised as a cleaning woman. Knowing that my ghetto side was a threat that could surface at any time, the agent was intuitive when he saw what happened to Michael.

"Under normal circumstances you'd be able to nurse Michael back to health, Frankie Mae. I saw you pass out back there, but you have got to get your damn ass together and get the fuck out of here. You'd be able to tell the world how much you love him and be there to watch him recover. Your man has been critically injured. I am telling you now to go home. I know you. I know how you feel about this man. I can't stand by and let you just go off here. So go home now," he ordered.

The agent was a big black guy. He was tall, bald, and weighed close to 320 pounds. I didn't give a fuck. I hauled my fist back as far as I could. I lunged forward, all 120 pounds of me, and nearly knocked the hell out of that man. Like an untamed lion, I came at his ass.

"I can't hide shit," I screamed. "I've been hiding shit for too long. They treat my baby like this. He knew something was the fuck wrong with this goddamn setup. You can do what the fuck you want to do, nigga, but I am not gonna leave him this way. Not today!" It was time to get ghetto, and I put my whole body and soul into this act. My body began to shift from left to right. I had snatched my wig off like I was getting ready for a street fight. Hell, all I needed was Sherry's razor-blades in my hair and it was on.

People were staring at me backstage. I heard one lady ask, "Who the fuck is that? Y'all get her ass out of here!" she shouted.

I wasn't going anywhere. I came out of the bag and just acted a complete fool in front of everybody over Michael getting hurt. "Let me see Michael!" I shouted, doing one of those ghetto back-and-forth moves with my chin. The kids were at my side now crying to see their daddy.

The agent stiff-armed me back away from the stage area. I couldn't move.

"Let go of me!" I shouted. "You let me see Michael, mutha-fucka! Let me see him now!"

That nosy lady came over to ask what was going on. "They're getting Michael ready to take him to the hospital. Fred," she said to the agent, "get this bitch out of here."

"This *bitch*?" I said, jumping in her face.

The woman checked out the hair, the face, the stance, and she left the stage.

"I got this, Grace," the agent called after her. The agent was going to hold me in this one spot until they took Michael out the back door safely. He couldn't do anything else. The agent knew if he went too far with me (as he did at that Four Seasons dinner) that Michael Jackson would kill him and that Grace bitch. I had heard Michael tell him more than once if he ever laid a hand on me the wrong way, he'd flat out kill his ass.

The agent took a deep breath as the commotion increased near the area where Michael had been hurt. The whole place was musky with smoke, as that Grace bitch cleared hundreds of people off the stage. Everybody was coughing by the time the fire department arrived. Still dressed in his show clothes, Michael was on a small stretcher telling his handlers to go find Frankie Mae. That Grace bitch told him there wasn't a Frankie here. They took what he was saying as delirium over the accident, because nobody knew a Frankie Mae. That name had never appeared anywhere in the media because nobody knew who the fuck Frankie was. They ignored him and kept pushing the stretcher to the exit, cosigning on what Grace was saying, as they sped out of the door to the waiting ambulance. I heard a family member tell him it was all going to be okay. When they brought the stretcher past me, that Grace bitch made sure it kept moving. All I could see was my baby holding up his glove with a white bandage wrapped tightly around his head. I was reaching out for him from behind the agent's back while Grace made sure that Michael Jackson did not see me.

"You can't," he said quietly, noticing the rebellion in my eyes towards Grace.

Next, the agent, a good man who knew every inch of my relationship with the King of Pop, hugged me on one side. Then he hugged my crying children on his other side. "I know how much you love him, baby, and I damn sure know how much he loves you. But I am trying to protect what you guys have. You must turn around at this very minute like this man you love knows you can. You must take your kids and leave. Grace is a stage manager. She is just doing her job. Loving him like you do, be glad she's got his back.

"Now, take a bus, take a cab, moonwalk if you have to, but leave before you cause a scene like you did that day at the restaurant. The minute the media finds out about you and the kids, I can assure you this, Michael will lose complete interest in maintaining the favor he has for you, Frankie Mae. I have been with Michael for enough years to know him. You might've gotten away with this shit that night with Michael. But he ain't here to protect you now, and these people don't know you from Adam. He expects you to be in control. Prove to him he was right when he fell in love with you."

The agent quietly walked me outside. "I'm gonna be honest with you, Frankie Mae. Michael told me you are one of the most special persons he ever met in his life. He told me you could get ghetto but he loves you this way. But I'm a have to have a talk with my man after today," he said, looking at me all funny. Even the kids were laughing now. I held my head down, feeling kind of guilty. I didn't mean to come out of the bag on blast. But this is my man we're talking about, and hell, I just had to go there with him and with Grace.

The agent could almost hear what I was feeling when he said, "Run. You must do what you have been doing since you met this superstar. Only now you must play your role better and grow the fuck up," he advised.

~~~

After the Pepsi disaster I became very ill. Michael Jackson's accident was much more serious than the media had reported. Michael had kept singing and dancing, never feeling his hair was smoldering into fire, yet he had suspected that things weren't right.

I only knew how bad it was when one of my sons screamed, "Mama!" My son had never screamed that loud before. Right then we all saw the red and orange flames that caused my man to suffer serious second- and third-degree burns on his head. After his departure, I didn't know when I'd see Michael again. What was to come later would leave people believing that this accident was the beginning of Michael's dependency on painkillers.

At work I sat through shifts I normally stood through, worrying about Michael. He had not called me in weeks. Loving him and knowing his pain was the hardest thing in the world to live through. At work I was short with Lita and coworkers because I didn't know what the agent had told Michael about my own Pepsi performance with Grace. The news had hit the covers of newspapers around the world. One ad showed me yelling at Grace, looking like a real crack addict. I prayed that my man would never see that photo. If he had, that could be the reason his calls had fallen off. It was hard working with people who knew you were acting strange and hiding something all the time.

After the accident, Michael's friends throughout
~~~

the media, including Liza Minnelli's fake husband, said Michael had changed. When I called Michael's cell phone and he didn't answer it, my only contacts were with the agent. I had never questioned the agent before, but I'd never forget what he said the day of Michael's accident. I was not going to start at this moment to forget the greatest lover of my life.

The Change in Michael Jackson

Using perfect timing, Michael called a few days after the accident. He told me he had to see me because the agent told him what had happened backstage with me and Grace and it worried him. He wanted me to see with my own eyes that he was all right, so I wouldn't hate Grace, he joked. Apparently Grace had been one of his staff members for many years. She found out how much I meant to Michael when he fired her after hearing how she talked to me from the agent. As soon as I got the call, I knew the routine. I ordered a disguise. A cab took the kids to be with a sitter and then one took me to the airport so I could go to the burn unit and see Michael.

From 1984 to 1987 I worked as much overtime as Lita could give me to get over Michael. The agent was calling me every day to tell me Michael was still trying to get over what happened at Pepsi, and because of these changes he couldn't take my calls. Our love was slipping into oblivion – but I was still committed to the relationship and was elated when Michael finally called. I read everything I could about him, and what I didn't know the kids came home and told me about. It was Shuun who told me he heard Michael was working on a new album between January and July of 1987. Now Shuun was twelve and little Daryle was five. Each of them wore the *Beat It* and *Thriller* jackets to stay close to Michael in spirit.

Michael called me one day to ask me what I thought of him hooking back up with Quincy Jones. Now our relationship had really turned into a friendship because of my performance at the Pepsi incident. It didn't hold too well with Michael because of what he'd had to do to protect me.

Despite that performance, Michael always trusted me. He respected my love for him and he respected my judgment. He might pout a little about my ghetto behavior, but it was never too long before he'd call me to get permission to do something.

Michael's hooking back up with Quincy Jones gave everybody the relief we had been looking for. Michael trusted Quincy and he knew that Quincy had his back. Michael wrote: "Bad," The Way You Make Me Feel," "Speed Demon," "Liberian Girl," "Another Part of Me," "I Just Can't Stop Loving You," "Dirty Diana," "Smooth Criminal," and "Leave me Alone."

One song on this album was one I was very familiar with because Michael had literally started writing "The Way You Make Me Feel," on my stomach one morning. I personally fell in love with "Bad" because to me that is what Michael made me feel like when I was with him, and he looked perfect on the white cover. Before "I Just Can't Stop Loving You" was released on July 27, 1987, I received another call from a healthy-sounding Michael.

"You want to come to the release party for your favorite song 'Bad'?" he asked me.

"You sure?"

"Well, if you don't cuss out the waitresses, yell at stage hands, or knock out three-hundred-pound agents with your cute little fist, I want you back," he chimed.

Now I knew why it had taken him so long to call

me after the Pepsi accident. Niggas. *What I say about niggas*, I thought. His team had obviously had a long talk with him about behavior. Michael told me never to change.

"I'll be there," I joked.

"Okay, the world release is on August 31, 1987. But you know I am gonna have to get me some before that," he said with glee. It was good to hear my man back to himself again and wanting to resume our love. It had been months since we'd had sex. I missed him and needed him. None of us told him he had been calling my name the day he was burned. The media bleeped it out. Nobody knew who Frankie was, and if they found out about it the wrong way, it could cost them their jobs.

When he told me Director Martin Scorsese was directing "Bad," I screamed into the telephone.

"Alright now, girl!" he reminded me. "You promised me you'd be good," he said cautiously. "I love you, Frankie Mae. I miss you so much I don't know how my heart beats without you around."

"You do love me?" I asked.

"Who knows why love is what it is, baby?" There was a long silence on the telephone. We were both crying. I was crying for love, crying for the changes to change, and wanting like hell to be near the set of "Bad." I was crying too because I couldn't wait to see him again.

For the whole six weeks it took for them to make the video that cost over two million dollars, I was with Michael Jackson. Seeing him in his element was indescribable. Now being with him took on a whole new feel as Michael Jackson had become the greatest entertainer in the entire world. If I was not with him physically, I was on the phone with him. Suddenly, a relationship that had been so tested seemed even more unreal to me. The only thing stronger than the love I felt for Michael was the power of the media to destroy him. Michael was on the phone with me asking me millions of questions about his new album. I answered all of his questions dutifully, and asked another million questions of my own. I was most proud of Michael's continued success, and inside I was very worried about my man's future.

Holding On

To love someone this deeply and see him suffer so badly on a television screen does murder to the heart. From "Bad" days onward, Michael never sounded the same to me when he called. He always sounded as if he was surrounded by puppets that told him everything he needed to say. Often now the agent would relay messages from Michael that didn't really sound like the things Michael would normally say to me in person. Remembering the first day we met, I prided myself on how good of a job Michael had done to protect and insulate our love. Had we not done it his way, what happened to Michael would have been even more devastating to us.

I often thought back to Michael's hospital stay after the Pepsi fiasco. I was so damn mad at that damn agent, I could even fool his ass. So, during Michael's hospital stay, I watched members of his family visit him at the hospital. I sat near most of them dressed like a bag lady, fooling even Michael's agent. The disguises were a trademark with Michael, and I had become a genius in creating and wearing them. In private we had thousands of them. Michael taught me and the kids how to wear the costumes and how to completely become another person simply by covering up in well-designed, colorful, illusive garb. I was at my man's side in the pitch of night.

The evening Michael called me on the fly after his

accident, I snuck into his room and it became one of the most memorable unions we ever had. Michael was in so much pain, he couldn't smile. I had to warn him to stop ringing the call bell for so much medication.

"It's hard to go through all this pain, baby," he told me. I rubbed his beautiful cheeks. He stayed hot. I brought in handheld fans to soothe his pain and steer him away from all the medication. I sat by his bed letting the fresh air blow onto his sore face. In these special quiet moments, Michael told me I felt like his wife.

"What would I do without you, ghetto girl?" he chimed.

"You'd have a sweet woman who didn't cuss and who did her nails," I answered.

My man tried to laugh and it hurt so bad he cried. "Don't do that again. Promise?" he asked.

I did it again. I would do anything to get him off of that Demerol drip and see him back to his old self again.

From then on, I snuck into his room and oftentimes just climbed my ghetto butt right up in the bed with Michael, and no one ever knew.

"I love you, baby. I'm sorry this is so hard for you," Michael said.

"I understand, Michael. Believe me, I understand," I promised.

Eventually Pepsi settled out of court with Michael. He gave over a million dollars to the Brotman Medical Center in Culver City, California, which now has a "Michael Jackson Burn Center."

Never Can Say Goodbye

Michael Jackson, 1985

In 1985, Michael Jackson was invited to the White House and was personally thanked by then-President Ronald Reagan at a White House ceremony for donating the song "Beat It" for use in television and radio public service announcements for drunk-driving prevention.

Jackson continued his charity work in 1985 by co-writing, with Lionel Richie, the hit single "We Are the World." The charity single helped to raise money and awareness for the famine in East Africa and was one of the first instances where Jackson was seen as a humanitarian. The song also won a Grammy Award for "Song of the Year."

Michael Jackson, 1987

"Bad" was a 1987 hit recording by American singer Michael Jackson. The song was the second of five Billboard Hot 100 number-one hit singles from the album *Bad* (the first time a recording artist achieved this feat) and was his seventh number-one single overall.

The song was originally intended as a duet with longtime rival Prince, which one can infer with the song's lyrics. Quincy Jones, in an interview included in the special edition of *Bad*, said that Prince told Jackson and him that he had not wanted to participate because "it would be a hit without [him]." In a 1996 interview with German TV, Prince also humorously said that the reason he didn't want to participate was the first line: "Your butt is mine." He said to Jackson, "I ain't saying that to you . . . and you sure ain't saying that to me!"

Michael Jackson, 1988

In 1988, Jackson released his first autobiography, *Moon Walk*, which took four years to complete and sold 200,000 copies. Jackson wrote about his childhood, The Jackson 5, and the abuse he had suffered. He also spoke of his plastic surgery, saying he had had two rhinoplastic surgeries and the surgical creation of a cleft in his chin. He attributed much of the change in the structure of his face to puberty, weight loss, a strict vegetarian diet, a change in hairstyle, and stage lighting. *Moon Walk* reached the top position on *The New York Times* Best Seller list. The musician then released a film called *Moonwalker*, which featured live footage and music videos that starred Jackson and Joe Pesci. *Moonwalker* debuted atop the *Billboard* Top Music Video Cassette chart, staying there for 22 weeks. It was eventually knocked off the top spot by *Michael Jackson: The Legend Continues*.

In March 1988, Jackson purchased land near Santa Ynez, California, to build Neverland Ranch at a cost of $17 million. He installed Ferris wheels, a menagerie, and a movie theater on the 2,700-acre (11 km^2) property. A security staff of 40 patrolled the grounds. In 2003, it was valued at approximately $100 million. In 1989, his annual earnings from album sales, endorsements, and concerts were estimated at $125 million for that year alone.

His success resulted in his being dubbed the "King of Pop." The nickname was popularized by Elizabeth Taylor when she presented him with an "Artist of the Decade" award in 1989, proclaiming him "the true king of pop, rock and soul." President George H. W. Bush presented him with the White House's special "Artist of the Decade." From 1985 to 1990, he donated $500,000 to the United Negro College Fund, and all of the profits from his single "Man in the Mirror" went to charity. Jackson's live rendition of "You Were There" at Sammy Davis Jr.'s 60th birthday celebration received an Emmy nomination.

The Promise
Michael Jackson, 1989

In 1989, Michael demonstrated his giving nature when he gave AIDS patient Ryan White a new Ford Mustang as a gift from a mysterious benefactor. I knew personally the gift was from Michael because our bed where we had found so much love and pleasure was a Ford Mustang. He did so many things the world was the last to know about. I gloated in the wonderful things Michael always did for others.

He had earned an enormous amount of money, and it was getting more difficult for him to let the kids and me live as we were living in Oakland, California. Michael Jackson was never embarrassed about my living situation or where I lived. It was love that made him want to include my family in his life. His annual earnings from album sales, endorsements, and concerts were estimated at $125 million for 1989. Around this time Michael became the first Westerner to appear in a television ad in the Soviet Union. So marked the talk of his everlasting title: "The King of Pop." When Michael called to tell me that Elizabeth Taylor had given him the name, I had to remind him that the Black community had already been calling him the King of Pop. I had referred to him as such early in our relationship. On the very day Michael and Elizabeth Taylor met at the White House during the George H. W. Bush administration, Michael called me from his private limousine to tell me the good news before the world knew what was going to happen.

"Are you going to spend any time with her?" I asked, referring to Elizabeth Taylor. I wanted to say bad things about her. Of all the women Michael Jackson was with or he told me about, I was skeptical of Elizabeth Taylor. She had married many times and she liked to save people. Michael didn't need saving, and I wanted him to stay as far away from her ass as he could.

"Frankie Mae, she's the first woman to demand a million dollars for a picture. She's—"

I cut my man off. I didn't talk bad to Michael often. But when I got mad, he knew to either listen or hang up the phone and never call me again.

"I don't care about her giving you the 'Artist of the Decade' award in front of the President, Michael. I don't trust this woman. Soon as the kitchen gets hot, Liz will act like she don't even know you, Michael."

"Look. Maybe you'll be happy to know they're honoring me from 1985 onward and I am gonna donate half a million dollars to the United Negro College Fund. I know how much these things mean to you," he stated. "All of the profits from 'Man in the Mirror' will go to charity. I can't do all of these things if I don't patronize stars like Liz and Liza."

"Baby, I like Liza Minnelli, but Liz has got to go. My mother loves the woman, but I ain't my mother. If we have to love the old bitches, I like Lana Turner. Why don't you find her and take her to some of these 'King of Pop' things?"

Michael laughed. He was smart not to take me seriously. I knew that Lana Turner was dead, but I was genuine when I told him I liked her a lot better than I liked Elizabeth Taylor.

My Favorite Album, *Dangerous*

Michael Jackson, 1990

When the '90s rolled around, Michael and I celebrated over ten years of love with two trips to the Bahamas, one trip to Hawaii, and three nights in Paris. By then Michael Jackson knew that *Dangerous* was to me his best album yet. He reminded me that I had said the same thing about *Bad*. But I convinced him that I liked *Dangerous* better than I did *Thriller* or *Bad*. By now people at work had a feeling that I was somehow involved in Michael Jackson's life. It was hard to hide the limousines that picked me up when Michael got into town or the emergency trips to Los Angeles, of which there were many. There were always neighbors standing outside waiting for Michael to show up. Keeping the relationship quiet was getting harder, but I was still holding it down. Most brothers like black women to be simple. Keep it clean and keep yourself fresh, but keep it simple.

When the *New York Times* said some horrible things about my favorite album, the record sales put those negative comments to shame. The kids and I were flown to the Super Bowl where millions watched Michael give one of his best performances at the 1993 Super Bowl halftime show.

A Tough Time for Love

The year 1993 was a tough period for both Michael Jackson and me. On February 10, 1993, Oprah Winfrey interviewed Michael Jackson in front of a reported 62 million viewers. We had talked about the interview and debated back and forth for hours on whether or not Michael should talk extensively to Oprah. My mother was sick, and at any time, Michael had agreed that he'd be with me if her health deteriorated. Michael, dressed in a beautiful red and gold outfit, told Oprah about his childhood, saying that being an entertainer had prevented him from having a typical childhood. This was something that Michael and I had talked about in great depth. He didn't need to go on Oprah for me to know how much he loved children. He told me he had to do this interview so people who wondered about his love for children would understand why he loved being around them.

I wished as I watched this interview that I could show the world what a great father Michael Jackson had been to my kids for years now. He had provided for them. He had changed diapers when my youngest boy was a baby. He made sure the kids were first in our relationship. That is not to speak of the tremendous donations Michael Jackson gave to help children of all ages He was a magnificent giver. He understood children so well because he was intrigued by the absence of his own youth. I understood that about Michael better than anyone.

My mother died in May 1993. Michael was there for me. He called to make sure the arrangements were like we wanted them to be. He offered to pay for the funeral, but our family told the great star this was something we wanted to do solely from a family perspective. Michael told me to put all of my differences aside regarding my family. Nobody believed that we were together until he marched into the services with me by his side. I had always wanted to tell everybody about Michael and our special relationship. Now, the time was right to do just that. The revelation was more sublime than anything. Some family members thought it was real; others thought it was merely a manifestation of my fantastic need to be a part of a great entertainer's life.

In August of that year, Michael Jackson was investigated by the Los Angeles Police Department after a thirteen-year-old boy lied, telling authorities Michael sexually abused him over four months. This time Michael defended against the charges, calling them extortion. A month later, the boy filed a civil suit against Michael accusing him of sexual battery, negligence, and fraud. As soon as I heard the charges, I checked myself into the hospital, believing Michael fully.

It was hard to understand the great lengths people would go to get their hands on Michael's fame and his money. I witnessed things in his life that had me wanting to shout out the truth from the Grand Canyon. I went crazy trying to understand why people were doing this to the most giving person I knew. Michael called me in the hospital asking me what I wanted him to do about all of this. I told him to settle. Do anything to get these evil people out of his life forever. As he sat by my bedside in the hospital, for the first time in the history of our relationship, all the work, concerts, and sharks had finally bitten into the psyche of my man and me. Soon Michael paid a reported $15 to $20 million to a begging shark just to see this all go away. And the whole time Michael Jackson was innocent of all these accusations, people were making big time money off the pain of one of the nicest individuals I ever knew.

Later things just got worse for Michael. He'd come to the apartment tired all the time. We had stopped having sex after all these child molestation charges, because Michael was understandably exhausted. The lies, the media, and the sharks had killed his spirit. The charges were filthy and dirty. After being hounded daily by these phony child-abuse charges, it started affecting both of us. I was missing work as a security guard and Michael missed concerts; he even canceled his tour in Mexico City. I had discussed it with Michael in detail after his appearance on Oprah. I told him to call his friend Elizabeth Taylor to get him help with all the medications he was taking just to go to sleep at night. When Michael came out in a public announcement on TV, my family supported him. I believed in Michael 100%. Nobody could endure the horrible things that I saw Michael go through over the years. In his statement, Michael told the world that he was addicted to painkillers and was seeking treatment.

Michael Jackson, 1995

In 1993 Michael was accused of abusing Jordan Chandler. Just months into Michael's very public death, these vultures would recant this sordid story of lies against Michael.

Jackson and Jordan had become friends in May 1992, at a time when we both met and liked the father and child. The father tried to push a movie script on Michael to give to Stephen King. When the deal fell through, the charges were born. I thought they were good people at first. There was no reason other than the eventual lies why Michael could not maintain a friendship with the boy and his father. The friendship became well known, but Michael had not become a member of the Chandler family unit as it had been reported. He merely loved children, and he attempted to do whatever he could to make sure life was easier for the sick and underprivileged.

I was with Michael when they said he did all of these horrible things to this child, and I can affirm they were all lies. And I was there when Evan Chandler was tape-recorded threatening to damage Michael's career. This man and his son lied to benefit from Michael's incredible generosity and success. It was the first time I ever saw how one-sided the media could let a story be. The whole thing sickened me, so I had to back out of my man's life to recover from the lies.

When the Neverland Ranch was made dirty by police, Michael told me he hated the ranch. The vultures had turned it into such an ugly place that he didn't want the kids and me there anymore.

Down for the Count

All of these charges and fabrications had Michael and me creating strategies and ways we could get back to being normal while avoiding the media again. Soon drugs became a regular relief mechanism for Michael, and I couldn't stop his need for this release. Still, I had never seen my man take a drug. I never believed his dependency had reached the stage that the media was reporting until Elizabeth Taylor went public to tell the world that she was helping her friend Michael with drug addiction.

The stress, on the other hand, was very real. When my man canceled his Dangerous Tour, we took many trips overseas. I got a call one night from him saying he was about to begin a relationship with Elvis Presley's daughter and were it not a part of our plan, being with the beautiful daughter of Elvis Presley and later marrying her would have sent me through the damn roof. Michael promised me continued love. Before long, the world and the media could see that Michael's heart was somewhere other than with Lisa Marie Presley.

If Michael had kissed me the way he kissed Lisa Marie publicly, our relationship would not have lasted one night, guaranteed.

This was a man I had given all these years to. I loved him. I was there for him at every turn, and the truth is, Michael's heart had long since been spoken for, but the world did not know that until now. Just as I had done before, I let it happen and stood right there offering my support, wishing I could put an end to the madness. When the government strip-searched Michael, he told me he felt his life was over, and I stood by his side telling him to be strong. By then his brothers had turned him on to the Koran. Suddenly, Michael had a better understanding of why these things were happening to him and why Mr. "M" didn't promote one of his best albums ever, *Dangerous*. We had a conference call where Michael told his friends and legal advisers we had to do something to bring this all to an end. Michael then settled the case. But to me the damage was done and the nightmare was only beginning to start.

Calling a Spade a Spade

When I entered into this long relationship with Michael, I already had a deep distrust for the entertainment business. I had written good books, some of them better than the trash I was picking up and buying right off the bookshelves. That's when I realized the world still has some kind of damn agenda against black people. By 1995, Michael was in deep turmoil with a jealous media who could not accept the fact that a black man had taken over the entertainment world hands down.

Now the media was out there trying to tear an innocent man down. The world didn't know it, but I knew that my man was turning into a victim of his success. I loved him too much to really break it all down to him, but I saw what was going on. I saw his once public friends like Elizabeth Taylor begin to waver in their support of Michael. It made me question whether or not slavery had come back to America.

Tabloid reaction to the allegations was so negative towards Jackson you almost believed all the lies they were reporting in the news.

According to Wikipedia, "Public polls at the time reported that a large majority of people believed Jackson was innocent."

Tarnishing a good man's image does more to the spirit than just taking a gun and shooting my man down to the ground. The public, who believes anything, believed that Michael was guilty of these abuse charges. I am going to tell you firsthand, calling a spade a spade, you got punk'd if you believe that Michael Jackson ever put his hand on a child wrong. No man on this planet cared more for the human spirit, children, and fairness than Michael Jackson. Period.

Perceptions from the side of the mass media remained. Michael had paid off the crooks, but the next time they would make sure that if Michael did not get convicted of the phony, salacious charges, they'd use an Uncle Tom nigga to drug my man up under the direction of the white man. They'd kill Michael Jackson one way or another while the damn coroner's office in Los Angeles would take their time calling the end of my man's life murder.

Here We Go Again, 2005

We had been through a lot together by the time Michael Jackson was found not guilty of all charges at the end of his four-month-long child abuse trial. There were daily telephone calls to me citing his innocence. It was an innocence I already believed in. My children and I showed up at the trial every day. We led the crowd with cheers outside of the court as the verdicts were read. Michael told me to forgive Gavin Arvizo for lying about him giving him alcohol and trying to kidnap him and his family. Of course it was all lies and had been the case a few years before. Our relationship had now become closer, as Michael and I both agreed we had done the right thing shielding our long relationship from the media. I believe to this day that had he not fired that lowdown bitch Grace, we would have been exposed.

The day the 2005 case was over, our family left Santa Maria, telling Michael not to speak publicly. I had talked to Thomas Mesereau, who declared that justice was served in Michael's innocence. He agreed with me, saying the less people knew about me the better. I loved the man and I thanked him profusely for defending Michael. As hundreds of fans showed up outside the ranch, Michael was completely exhausted. I offered to get on the plane and go home to Oakland, but he would not have it.

Now that it was all over, everybody was relieved. The whole time this ordeal was happening, I asked myself why Michael would put himself through all of this agony for superstardom. Our decision to keep our relationship secret had been the right choice at every turn, but some people, like my boss Lita, refused to be fooled. Michael had been through so much during the trial, and when I looked around and saw Lita and my coworkers rooting for Michael, I knew we had been found out.

I got more calls from him in emergency rooms than ever before. I wanted so badly to reach out to his family and the people who were closest to Michael, but by now I didn't know who to trust. I blamed everybody for Michael's predicament. When Judge Rodney Melville told Michael he could go home after the verdict, I didn't know if he'd personally jump up and snap handcuffs on his hands. My kids and I felt like the jury who had vindicated Michael. They had asked to be returned to their private lives anonymously, and the kids and I shared that sentiment, still worrying how all of this was going to affect Michael Jackson in the end. I was glad the jury had judged Michael as a human being and not on his enormous celebrity status. They did for Michael what I had been trying to do for him since the day we got together. I looked at him as just another individual, not a celebrity. That thinking kept our love real and fluid for many years. Not seeing him for days, months, and years had indeed been a fair tradeoff to preserve a love he needed in his life.

When reporters and supporters gathered for the verdicts, the redheaded guy who tried to finger me at work aimed his camera at me again. This time he winked at me and for a second time, he passed on taking my picture. I was ever so grateful to those who respected my privacy with Michael, but especially this redheaded guy who worked for *People Magazine*. When fans cried as the decisions were cited to the world, I was just thankful that Michael was going to be able to go back home to the family and fans who loved him.

Some fans believed that the justice system had been vindicated by the fair verdict for Michael. To me it was all a death sentence.

Newsweek, July 13, 2009, said, *"Before Michael Jackson came Frank Sinatra, Elvis Presley, and the Beatles; after him has come absolutely no one."*

On June 25, 2009, the world mourned the death of Michael Joseph Jackson, and that was the day that I literally went crazy. From my living room in East Oakland, I was forced to take a look back at my life. I sat on the red sofa, rocking like a madwoman with tears raining down my face as I went way back to remember Michael Jackson.

~~~

In 1962 I was seven years old when my father remembered Joseph Jackson before the Jackson fame. During a dinner conversation with my family, formerly from Gary, Indiana, Daddy bragged that his friend from Gary called my great-aunt Pat a friend of his and Katherine's. My father laughed at how well Michael's father led his crew as a steel crane operator. Joseph liked my father back then. In fact, Joe (as workmates called him) relied on his advice at work for many things. He helped many of his friends get jobs in Gary. Like my father, and like most fathers from the Civil
~~~

Rights era, Joseph Jackson spent what little break time he had discussing a positive, flourishing future for his family. Michael even bragged about how Joseph and Katherine would wake them up at all hours to see James Brown on Ed Sullivan.

When Joe discovered Michael's incredible talent at an early age, he shared it with his coworkers, saying he was going to make it one day. Based on the fantastic man Joe was at work, Daddy said he told a select group of workers back then that if it wasn't him, then he'd find success for his talented boys, for sure. Everybody believed Joseph would make it. They said, "You judge a man by his hard work and his good deeds." On those accounts, Joseph Jackson delivered. And nobody was surprised when his dream of success for his boys became real.

By 1968, while Michael Jackson was a ten-year-old boy signing a Motown contract with Barry Gordy, I was a thirteen-year-old girl discovering how cool it was to be black and proud via James Brown. When Michael came out with "I Want You Back" a year later in 1969, that was the end of my James Brown, jerking-with-the-music, afro-loving days. It was also the beginning for Michael Jackson and his brothers. Michael was about to launch a career that would supersede one of our idols, James Brown.

I was in love now (like everybody else) with Michael Jackson! And I would remain in love with him until his sad final days.

Needless to say, Joseph Jackson fulfilled his dream. It was Joseph and his wife who created Michael, Marlon, Tito, Jermaine, Jackie, and later Janet Jackson; the group of the late '60s was the team we came to love as the Jackson 5.

Suddenly, as I looked at the TV screen, it was 1978 when Michael and Diana Ross starred in *The Wiz*. The movie would have been a hit, but nobody liked Diana Ross for the role of Dorothy. We talked about the movie in beauty shops and clubs – wherever groups of African Americans met. We hoped the talented pint-sized Stephanie Mills would get the role. People argued that Diana Ross was too old to be playing the kid Dorothy, who was trying to find her way back home to Kansas City.

Stephanie Mills, whose biggest hit was *Home*, was a huge talent out of the '70s. She appeared as a guest on popular TV shows and she had a voice that was perfect for *The Wiz*. Our popular choice for the role lost out to Diana's friendship with Michael.

Michael Jackson was perfect as the scarecrow, and Nipsey Russell was great as the tin man, but it was no surprise to anyone in the black community that *The Wiz* bombed at the box office. Diana Ross had many successes as a singing superstar and even as an award-winning actress, but she was to me the sole reason that *The Wiz* failed.

Not long after *The Wiz* bombed in 1979, my husband of one year died of liver cancer. My husband loved Quincy Jones. His favorite song from Michael Jackson's *Off The Wall* album was "Rock with You." It was played at his funeral. He'd never live to see the day that his wife would meet and fall in love with his favorite superstar.

Today, faced with the reality that Michael, my father, and my former husband are dead, I went into denial about Michael's death, making tons of videos on YouTube and not knowing what day it was or what time had passed. Michael gave me great memories as I reached out to his spirit, looking for ways that I could memorialize my man's great deeds in a fun and positive way. Nothing made me feel better about Michael Jackson's early, early death.

So, I leaned on what I do best. I wrote about my feelings in a heartfelt fantasy that could have been any of ours, and I would leave it up to the reader to determine the truth of my words. I created and believed in my heart that at one time during his life I had become a special love to Michael J. Jackson. Be it real or be it fantasy, I loved Michael Jackson.

Today, whereas I may truly need therapy to get over Michael, he was and is the greatest love and world entertainer that I have ever known. *The Love He Saved* belongs to all young girls or any fan who posted a picture on her wall believing one day she'd meet and fall in love with Michael Jackson. This story is for any little girl who ever dreamed she could be the one for Michael Jackson. This story is your fantasy, too.

At the end of this book you will read about the many organizations Michael Jackson gave freely to. To maintain the positive memories I have of this great entertainer, I encourage you to keep his legacy alive by loving him. Feel free to hold this memoir to your chest as yours. Love it and love him. For what happened to the little ghetto girl "Frankie Mae" could have easily happened to you. Read this book, enjoy it, and honor his great deeds forever.

To explain the depth of this fantasy love that I feel for this miraculous star, I spared nothing in presenting him to you as the perfect everyday handsome guy he was, my true life love fantasy.

~~~

Looking back on our relationship now, I remember that we had one of our biggest telephone fights when he left the "Soul Train" after-party with Brooke Shields in 1987.

"We have been together all these years!" I shouted at Michael Jackson over the phone. "I remain the little ghetto secret, not changing a thing, and you leave a black event with her!" I screamed, referring to Brooke Shields.

Michael Jackson had explained it to me repeatedly over the years that his friendship with Brooke Shields was 100% platonic. I had been dating him for years now and said nothing as the agent dragged my ghetto ass to the limo, then to the airport where I was deported
~~~

home. Before the plane landed, Michael had called to tell me never to come to an event where he was at without an invitation. Then he apologized for hurting my feelings. Again, he was the most considerate individual I'd ever met. Remember, his was the high world I rejected at all costs. Mine was the low one that gave Michael relief from never-ending industry demands.

Even when things got tougher in my fantastical relationship with Michael Jackson, I stopped at nothing to protect our relationship or to give the public something that is clearly running amiss in the media – the truth about Michael Jackson. I remember his incredible performance at the Super Bowl in 1993. That year tested our relationship. Jealousy and greed threatened to disturb Michael's clean image, and he did everything from going on Oprah to doing live statements to defend his reputation. I was devastated. While Michael was on tour in the Middle East, police threw me out of the house to scour the compound. I threw myself against the heavy gold doors, trying to stop security from letting them in. When I told Michael how awful this intrusion was, he was hurt. Michael ended his tour as all of this began to take a toll on my man. That was the day Michael Jackson hated Neverland. He told me in a phone call that he never wanted to go back to Neverland again.

Plagued with sleeping problems, Michael wanted to protect his children and all children. He wanted to provide a wonderful place of refuge for those he loved and his fans, never dreaming that the city would come into his house to violate his privacy, tearing down all the good things he had built in his home for others.

During the turbulent times we both held our breath, hoping Oprah, who never missed a link, would not latch on to his long relationship with me.

The Dangerous World Tour was Michael's second tour as a solo artist, covering Europe, South America, and Asia from June 27, 1992, to November 11, 1993. The tour was sponsored by Pepsi-Cola and it included sixty-nine concerts to four million fans. Michael and I argued three times over all those concert dates and wardrobe changes. One black, gold, and silver outfit he wore on the tour weighed forty-five pounds. I told him by the second leg of this tour he'd be hospitalized or dead if he kept going at this pace. In a meeting with handlers, Michael insisted that all profits from the Dangerous Tour be donated to his charities.

From one concert to another, Michael's sleep problems worsened, and you'd have to see all the physical work that went into this tour to believe the demands it placed on my man's body. Some of the dancers complained they could not keep up with Michael because he'd forget the steps.

The dance manager pulled a dancer aside, telling him, "If Michael changes a step, fall in or fall out. You follow Michael or quit."

The dancer dried sweat from his brow with a white cotton towel. Next he pushed his way off stage and left.

Michael was a quick dancer. He was gifted, and I had never appreciated how hard it was for professional trained dancers to keep up with the King of Pop. What I was seeing during this Dangerous Tour was nothing short of unbelievable. Michael would go on stage weighing 120 pounds and come off weighing 110 pounds, and some of the dancers simply collapsed backstage. As his woman, I could do nothing but wait for him and cry over what I was seeing. I met him backstage in 1993 where we decided together to end the Dangerous Tour.

"This is going to kill you, Michael. You're dehydrated and you look sick. You're older now and you can't do all the things you did ten years ago. You can't deal with all of this and these crazy abuse charges," I warned him.

Michael drank 24 ounces of vitamin spring water, sucking in deep breaths. The other performers exited the stage exhausted. Rounds and rounds of applause proved it was all worth the effort, but the reality of seeing Michael and these dancers after one of these performances was unreal.

"Frankie, let's not go there again. I am doing this world tour for the charities. Why do we have to keep having the same argument all the time?" he yelled. I knew him well enough now not to push the issue.

He had lost so much weight I hardly recognized him. After that particular concert I left without saying another word. Three days later, the agent sent the jet to

Oakland for me when Michael said he'd have to go to the hospital but he wanted to see me first. I came back, refusing to tell Michael, "I told you so." As things got worse, every two or three hours Michael popped painkillers, and I had never seen him take a pill before until now. He was so tired he could barely stand up in the hotel where we were staying. His friend, Elizabeth Taylor, stayed on the telephone with him, urging him to get help for the painkillers. He suffered from terrible headaches and would lie down just long enough to lose all of his energy in the next show.

We had thought the Dangerous Tour would allow MJ to focus on giving the fans good music. Hours of hard work and training dancers went into this tour. Michael and I went over songs, outfits, and the fan pleasers, with me begging him to tone it down. He strived to make sure Dangerous was a memorable affair for all of his fans around the world, but the bad people were determined to kill Michael Jackson. I was proud of him anyway, as I was stunned to see the determination of opportunists and the media to bring Michael Jackson down.

During the hardest times of our union, it just seemed like the world wanted to tear the nation's greatest entertainer down in front of his fans, and that hurt Michael Jackson more than anything.

For years I had been tucked into a crowd by the agent who told me not to start anything. By 1993 and during the Super Bowl performance, our long love relationship was almost ten years old. As I began to fade away with thousands of fans, Michael honored my love and my being there for him. In minutes his familiar gloved hand reached into the thick crowd for me.

"You ain't getting away that easy, Frankie Mae," he said, pulling me up to his VIP seats.

~~~

"I will be performing the songs my fans want to hear," Michael Jackson promised as he introduced the "This Is It" Tour. It was a tour the world would never see, for Michael died in June just a month before what would have been the greatest tour of all.

As time progressed from the '80s to the turbulent years of 1993 through 2005, there was nothing I could do to protect Michael from the bad people who spun him into public spectacles that nearly ruined his entire career. AEG and others sliced into his grand repetition, pushing him into one more performance. I had witnessed what one more performance was doing to the King of Pop. I cried because they didn't see the toll that one more performance had on his mind, his health, and his soul.

Such events drove him to a stronger dependency to use and to become numb to the world, like I knew he wanted to be in private. No doubt, the vultures were out to get Michael Jackson for one reason: money, period. They never cared that at the end of the day; even Michael Jackson was merely one human being.
~~~

While Michael struggled to make money for AEG and the vultures, Diana didn't even show up at the memorial, which I have a difficult time forgiving her for. She said publicly she loved Michael Jackson and that he was her friend, but she said that about Florence Ballard, too. I never believed Diana Ross, period. Elizabeth Taylor had married so many men – her credibility regarding love and men was shot with me until I heard her begging Michael Jackson to get help during his Dangerous Tour. Elizabeth Taylor crawled out of her sick bed and into her wheelchair to brave the heat in Glendale, California, to be at Michael's funeral, and I have nothing but respect for her now.

They said Diana Ross did not appear at the memorial or the funeral. I will never forgive Diana Ross for what she did to Florence Ballard of the Supremes. One only needed to see that picture of Florence Ballard on the cover of *Jet* magazine eating spaghetti and applying for food stamps to realize that being kicked out of a world-famous girls group in her prime had not been a picnic.

In 1983, when Michael Jackson called me and the kids from backstage at Motown 25, he told me Diana Ross was turning into a bitch diva when she pushed one of the Supremes and it was caught on tape. Some viewers saw it live on television. The producers bleeped it out, but the world had known for decades that Diana Ross was a self-serving bitch, and when Michael Jackson died she was still a bitch to me. Apparently nothing had changed.

Elizabeth Taylor and Diana Ross were two huge figures Michael loved openly. He respected some people who in my opinion did not deserve his respect. In honor of his greatness, they should have had "they" ass (as we say in the ghetto) at the damn funeral with bells on their toes for what Michael Jackson had done for them.

From 2005 onward I watched bad people take advantage of a good man. Because Michael Jackson's heart was huge, these bad people hurt my great love in ways that were unimaginable. Each lie took another piece of Michael's beautiful heart. Seemingly, after the knife went in, the bad guys just kept stabbing my man until they literally stabbed him to death. When you love somebody the way I love Michael Jackson, to watch these kinds of things happen affects your life, too. I am going on the record to say: "My life will never be the same without Michael Jackson on this planet."

Whereas I wanted to protect the man I loved, I was to the conventional world merely a crazed, uncouth fan. I was a little-known woman who loved Michael Jackson so much that the word "fan" diminished how I felt about the man. To this day, I am glad I never took a dime from Michael Jackson. What he gave us had no price tag attached to it.

So, there was little I could do once the wolves moved in to damage Michael's good deeds and his great name. At night I just held pictures of him to my breast, loving him, and today I look at his pictures with pride, knowing that he died so gracefully. Whereas the world wanted to see one more show, I wanted to see Michael Jackson in peace.

Evil formed a nexus to drive Michael Jackson down a dangerous path of drug use that eventually led him to his grave. He paid off the liars; he held on to the memories of fading friends. Michael walked through the shame of one lurid accusation after another. Where were his friends?

I watched all of this from afar, wanting to sacrifice everything I owned to be there for my man. The trials were nothing more than a sick public scheme – a modern-day witch hunt – to expose an innocent man for crimes he never committed. I cried, I cried, and I cried.

They ran him to Ireland, to Bahrain, and to London, away from his beloved country. In 2005 I was so glad the jury saw through the lies, ending this fiasco with a "not guilty" verdict. Jurors told reporters after the trial that they had relied on the facts of the case to vindicate an innocent man. Michael Jackson then wore a pain that the public could not fully see or understand. After 2005, Michael Jackson's heart was irreparably broken in a way that only those close to him could see.

Ultimately, when Michael died it was too late for the bad guys to take back what they had done to him. Even the bad guys went public to apologize for some of the lies that drove Michael Jackson to an untimely death. AEG waved money in the faces of the Jackson family, quieting even the most defiant family members like Jermaine. AEG made a deal to sell Michael higher in death than in life. Some family members wanted to put Michael back on the Neverland Ranch, the last place in the world that Michael Jackson wanted his soul to rest.

While it is said that the family was more interested in protecting Michael's legacy than making money off him, by August 21, 2009, AEG's petition to license a Michael Jackson memorabilia tour was granted. My heart sank. The crying got worse as my worst nightmare had come true. If Michael Jackson was worth more in death than in life, AEG had motive to kill Michael Jackson. When the news media boasted that the three-city tour could earn $6 million, I was inconsolable.

As I piece together Michael Jackson from the time I met him up to his death, I wish I could have done more to put a stop to the train wreck ahead.

One need only to have looked at him walking slowly into the courtroom, in blue pajama bottoms, black loose house shoes, hair disheveled, and heavily medicated, turning his head from side to side, needing the arms of strong agents to support his every step. During the whole trial, Michael Jackson had been off limits to all except his agents, who had little power over him, as they kept everyone – even Michael's own father – from getting close to him. I went crazy seeing how the lies and the trials did irreparable damage to a kind man who'd never had anything to do with hurting an innocent child.

Those who set out to ruin Michael drove a decent,

loving man, the world's most incredible talent, a multi-platinum superstar, to an untimely, unbelievable death, and this fan who loved him dearly is livid about it.

Michael Jackson succeeded in many ways despite the bad people's ongoing efforts to ruin his life. He is the King of Pop. He is the world-record breaker. His is the only human death we simply can't reconcile. Several months have passed now and much has been said about Michael Jackson. But I take my feelings for this man to the third degree. As a writer, I want to go down in history loving Michael Joseph Jackson and flat out denying any charge that Michael would ever hurt an innocent child. And ain't nobody gonna take that away from me. I had called Michael Jackson's death murder after the Dangerous Tour. To me the name Michael Jackson means eternal love for the entire human race. I will not forgive the bad people that killed Michael Jackson.

Never Can Say Goodbye

On the same day Michael Joseph Jackson and I were rejoined in love, we had planned it from the moment we first met on the Santa Monica Freeway, many years ago. When Michael died to the world, I was only a month away from my fifty-fourth birthday. Hours before his passing, I had taken a trip to Vegas.

In 2008 we celebrated the twenty-fifth anniversary of *Thriller* in Vegas. Michael called me and the kids while we were staying at Bally's, excited about the "gold" package that included new remixes, a DVD, and an unreleased song, "For All Time." Before his exit he was going to join us there to give me plans on where I'd meet him in London for the upcoming "This is It" Tour. Earlier in the day I received my regular telephone call from Michael, throwing away all of my bad memories regarding the Dangerous World Tour. He said rehearsals were going well for the big tour in London.

But over the past few months, he had told me the plans were constantly changing. It was obvious that 2005 had a noticeable effect on Michael and these changes made his inability to sleep worsen, and sadly, I knew all the reasons why. In spite of all that, Michael assured me he was ready for the tour. However convincing his voice seemed, Michael Jackson was not ready for the "This Is It" Tour. While he continued talking, I just loved hearing happiness in his voice. He told me tonight he was doing this tour for his kids, for the fans, and for the world that loved him.

After the trial we brushed over his known sleep problems, preferring to discuss living plans that promised renewal for Michael. He was tied up completely now with AEG and new handlers I didn't know. It was more difficult for me to get in touch with a man I had loved now for over twenty years.

That said, I could never forget the day when Michael Jackson told me he wanted to die young like Elvis. In the last five years, I had gotten used to being satisfied just hearing his voice and being as close as I was to Michael Jackson. I knew the day he went before the world to announce the tour that somehow he was not going to be there to start one song. It's a hard truth to come out with, and at this very minute I am soaked with tears. But my feelings of that time are no less than true. June 2009 he sounded upbeat on the telephone, but the sleep problem had a history going back decades and had become the topic of many conversations. Who knew one day the world would be concerned over something I had already known for decades. Michael Jackson had a terrible time getting sleep. Overall, he was happy about the upcoming tour in London and I had to convince myself hard that this was really true.

~~~

June 25, 2009, 5:00 p.m.

The world was mourning the death of the King of Pop Michael Jackson, as I leaped out of memories into immediate denial. Denial had been a constant companion throughout my relationship with Michael. Even at the very moment that Michael Jackson had come home to me, just as he had always promised me he would, I could not believe he was really knocking at the door right now.

I was back from Vegas sleeping on the new red sofa Michael had given me for my fifty-fourth birthday on May 12, knowing that our pact in life would succeed his death at any moment. I answered the door in my apartment in Concord, California, looking good, wearing my hair in the cornrows Michael loved seeing me in. I was also wearing one of the many white strapless dresses that he had bought me over the years. I was still a size six and he still had a better shape than I. Six was the same size I was when I met Michael, when he told me he had fallen in love with an old class picture he saw of me on Market Street in San Francisco.

Strangely, I was not crying. Quietly, for the moment I was relieved that the living body of Michael Jackson was finally at rest. It was a very hot summer day in Concord, California. I worried because I knew Michael hated hot weather. It was easier to see peace after assassination by the media, after all those hard rehearsals and after being the object of so many bad
~~~

people's self-serving purposes. No more court battles, no more tawdry accusations to destroy my man, and no more new handlers to keep him away from me. Today, this evening, Michael Jackson came home to me.

When he walked through the front door without his agent, I told him to sit down in his favorite beige lounge chair. He sat. He was quiet as I remembered our early days together when he came home to chirping children, who simply wanted him to make red Kool-Aid for them and to tuck them into bed. He always reminded me of two things: to believe and to be nice. I could get ghetto, and no one knew that better than Michael and the agent. I put up with his fame, his absence, his fans, and his women. Michael put up with my getting in his handlers' faces and my ongoing jealousy over women. I only did the ghetto thing on an emergency basis, when the forces worked to keep my man away from me.

Today, Michael Jackson was physically gone; but spiritually, Michael was home in an undisturbed peace.

The kids – Shuun, now 34, and Daryle, now 28 – called to see if I was okay over my man's death. I had been strong throughout my long relationship with Michael Jackson. I had seen him die many times on the road and in the media, even in rehearsal. There had been tougher times in life to deal with than now during his physical death. I told my grown kids to just leave me be. I assured them I was waiting for Michael to come home. They offered to come. I told them to let me mourn Michael in peace, alone.

Both my kids were inconsolable over Michael's death. They kept crying. One even wanted to go to Los Angeles and see the body before he believed the death.

Michael had been just like a father to them for over 28 years. Over the years he had told them bedtime stories. He featured them in our home videos and loved them by making them red Kool-Aid and kissing them goodnight. They were the first to see the moonwalk and the last to tell him, "I love you."

We had had numerous affairs over the years, and Michael had made sure that the kids were involved in his life, however secret it may have been. There were private meetings, costume changes. There was me going off on people who tried to put their digs into my man. There was trickery here and there to dodge the media or his family, even sometimes to dodge his wife or girl of the time. Sometimes it was fun. Sometimes hiding was rough and ever so tiresome. I never complained, but I did have to put my dukes up a couple of times. I followed the plans of Michael or his agent, doing whatever it took for me to be in my man's life except for taking his money or using his fame for personal gain. My children loved Michael Jackson. They had believed in him like I did 100%.

A Sad Goodbye

Fantasy took denial to a new front-page position in my heart today. The shock of losing Michael Jackson could not be tolerated in my waning heart. The words, "He's not dead," sat at the forefront of my consciousness, forcing me to continue to live my life with and not without Michael Jackson. For all that he meant to my tortured soul, I could not let him go.

Today we watched one of Michael's favorite television shows, *Family Feud.* I smiled when Michael Jackson, wearing a red flannel shirt with a gold military collar, got all the answers right. On other channels on a different set, there was wall-to-wall coverage of Michael Jackson's death. We had an understanding that all the *great* things they were saying about my man were true; but again, that was just the media preparing for tomorrow. The minute somebody mentioned lies we flipped the channel, and I told Michael what a shame it was for the media to prepare for his death when it was so far off.

Ignoring the news, today we sat on my red birthday couch holding hands, as I tried to forget what happened four years ago at his trial. Today, I kept wishing they'd quit comparing his death to Elvis Presley's. We looked at all the coverage quietly, with me appreciating a rare peaceful moment with my man. Here and now I wished that racism would die already in America. Soon Michael turned the channel when he saw Larry King asking Jermaine if Katherine Jackson was going to raise his kids as Jehovah's Witnesses.

When he saw his mother crying, tears streamed down Michael's face. He leaned forward with his black tresses covering the sides of his tired, bland face. Next, Michael cried. I had never seen him this hurt before. I patted him on the back knowing this was his moment. I leaned back on the couch and then patted him again on the back. Soon, he reached back and squeezed my hand, letting me know he loved me. Today I felt the same way about my man as I did back in the '80s when we met.

My kids were not the young kids who watched our love grow into what it was today. I remembered the night Michael moonwalked on Motown 25. He had called that night to make sure we were wearing our beaded gloves and watching the show. He also had called to confirm that I liked the jazzy black and silver outfit he was wearing for this life-changing event.

Today, my grown children respected our last day together. Real or imagined, this last day, this last moment, belonged to only Michael and me.

Thinking back to 1983 and the first day of Michael's incredible world success, I remembered handing the telephone to both children, who called him Daddy. We couldn't believe that in just minutes our hero would set the world on fire with the introduction of his much-talked-about moonwalk!

Michael, my man, my love, was disappearing before my very eyes. To the world he had already succumbed to death. To me he was sitting in the living room giving me my private moment to say goodbye. Then, suddenly, twenty-eight years of love seeped out of my body. I had kept this love harnessed through concerts, trials, backstage trauma, trials, everything. Michael's other relationships with women meant nothing to me, for I was never placed on the back burner of his life. Now all that I had held inside from family, from friends, from my job, from the agent, and from the public came out of my small frame into one loud shrill.

The Reality of Michael's Death

"Don't go, Michael," I screamed. We had been sitting together on the couch holding hands until he began fading before my very eyes. His strong grip changed from real to light until there was nothing. Now, just like in "Thriller," he began to change before my very eyes. Little by little, Michael Jackson was now leaving me.

"From the cake way to Broadway glory, you're watching *TV Guide*. As the world mourns the death of superstar Michael Jackson . . ." The TV kept saying he was gone. I began screaming for him to come back to me. It was too soon to let him go now. "*TV Guide* will give you the most comprehensive coverage of the legendary life of the King of Pop."

"Baby, please?" I begged. "Where are you, Michael?" I screamed, looking throughout my place frantically. Michael was gone. Just a moment ago he was sitting right next to me. Was I fucking crazy? Or was I simply a blind woman watching my life from an out-of-body view?

If the limo was parked outside in the same place the agent had parked for years, I would know I was not crazy. With that, I ran to the door looking for assurance. I searched the bare streets looking for the black limo that had always brought Michael home to me. At the curb, I looked up and down the street, wondering where the agent had gone. As I put my hands on my head to silence the pressure building at my temples, my dress drifted down, nearly exposing my bare breast. Shocked, I pulled it back up fast as I ran back upstairs to beg him not to leave.

"No! No! Don't do this to me, Michael. Please, please don't go. Don't leave me this way." Suddenly I said, "GOD!" Then, out of nowhere, God took over the wheel.

Again, I saw Michael Jackson's familiar, lean body glean back onto the couch where he had been sitting only minutes ago before he vanished. I sat there thanking God. I promised the Lord that I'd never forsake his name again for giving me another moment with Michael Jackson. Now the TV Guide channel showed Michael's brother Jermaine. Dressed in white and yellow, Jermaine was at a podium outside of a Los Angeles hospital. He said, "My brother, the legendary King of Pop . . ." and I turned the TV off before he could say another word.

Next, I heard Michael Jackson's voice again for the very last time. He said, "It's okay, baby. You'll see me again one day. Let me go. Don't you dare mess with an impersonator," he quipped, referring to a time when my boss had accused me of dating the superstar. "Aren't you glad that now you can talk about it?"

I looked around the empty living room, seeing nothing, but hearing everything he was saying to me. I panicked. Then I dropped to my knees. "Michael, I don't want to talk about it to anyone," I said real fast. "Come back, baby. Don't you leave me. You know I can't live without you. It's too early, Michael. I want you back. Don't leave me, baby, please," I screamed, pounding my fist into the red couch.

The phone rang. I knew it was the kids, so I didn't answer it. Then the cell phone rang, and I didn't answer it, either. It was going to take a long time for me to get over Michael Jackson's death. But while I was talking about it, I would leave no stones unturned and I would do everything humanly possible to bring him back to me. I went from delirious to calm. I'd jump all sides of the fence to bring Michael back.

"Haven't I been good to you? I have kept this love right here in my bosom for over twenty-eight years, Michael. After London we could have retired, baby. I don't want fame. I never took your money, your houses, or your cars because I need you, Michael," I screamed, emphasizing the word "Michael."

"Please, please come back . . ." I begged. "Come back! Don't you know how hard it was for me to see them take you away? I had that nigga pushing me into a wall when you got burned on that Pepsi set!" I shouted, referring to the agent.

Michael always laughed when I told him about that ghetto scene with the agent. Right now I heard nothing. Panic didn't work. Calm rendered less.

Next, I dropped to my knees and began banging my head into the floor, until blood dripped slowly from my lips. Later, I got up and grabbed a vase. I tore through the house breaking glass, ripping curtains and blinds to the floor. I cried; I cussed. I had never expressed pain concerning Michael before, not like this. I hid the relationship from everybody like a pro. But I couldn't hide my love with his leaving me before my very eyes. Not this time. I had known this was going to happen if they didn't leave him alone. I was inconsolable. As blood painted the white carpet in the living room red, I was gone.

I must have been sitting in one spot for two days waiting for Michael. When I regained consciousness, I lifted my head up from a pool of dried blood on the kitchen floor. I looked into my cell phone to learn that for the first time in our twenty-year relationship, neither Michael nor his agent had called me. Upon this recognition, I had to stop myself from going back to the abyss.

Today was June 27, 2009. He would have wanted me to get myself together for my young son's twenty-seventh birthday on June 28, 2009. The cell phone was loaded with calls from my kids. There was nothing from Michael or the agent. I could not let my kids see how devastated I was over Michael Jackson's physical passing.

I had waited for him one time for almost two years to come back to me. He always came back. Now he was gone forever at a time when our love had only just begun.

The Reality of Michael Jackson

As the world honored my dearest love Michael Jackson, I got myself back together well enough to recite our vows quietly in the sanctuary of my home. Crazy or not, to me he was there, otherwise today there would be no me. And, as crazy as I had become, this was the only way I could deal with Michael's death. The gravity of his leaving was too much for me to bear. Over the years he had sedated the ghetto side with his goodness and he watched the woman in me evolve. Soon I learned that his death was even worse for his family, for the world.

I had pretended when he was alive that he was not with Brook Shields and Webster and Lisa Marie Presley. I let them roll his body right past me on one of the worst nights in his life. I was not all that cool, but I did keep it together better than I was doing now. At the funeral I kept thinking of how I could preserve Michael's life. I wanted to create a way to honor his memory in the most positive way imaginable. Creating this book, *The Love He Saved*, turned out to be the cathartic chance for me to tell the world how much I loved Michael Jackson without ever having to let him go. Each fan should read this book and embrace *The Love He Saved* as his or her very own.

Today I could do what I wanted with him. There was no longer anyone here who could take Michael Jackson away from me again. If he was gone in the physical, hell, I'd bring him back to life for all of us as one love. You are cordially invited to the wedding of Michael Jackson and Frankie Mae.

Ceremoniously

"Do you take this lovely woman, Frankie Mae, to be your lawfully wedded wife, Mr. Jackson?"

"I do."

"Then you may kiss the bride."

He kissed me as fervently as he had done when he was alive. I looked pretty that day. My hair was right in a braided French roll the way Michael Jackson said he liked it. For the first time ever, I wore beautiful white makeup to match a beautiful white knee-length lace dress with white open-toe lace sandals. Michael was wearing the white suit he had on the *Thriller* album. Only I had made him wear the white shirt instead of the black one today.

I had instantly shut myself off to the world for a ceremony I could not deny between the two of us. I called my job I had been on for over twenty years as a security guard and told them the truth. "There's a death in the family, Lita. I don't know when I am coming back to work," I said before slamming down the phone.

I had always been the quiet type at work. Over the years I had lied and covered up my relationship with Michael Jackson royally. My guess was I had been completely successful in fooling the world over my very special relationship. I worked myself up from back-door security guard to front-desk security diva. Not one person on my job or in my private life, other than my immediate family and God, knew about Michael Jackson. If they knew, they never brought it up to my face. That said, my changed disposition prompted my supervisor Lita to call me right back.

"Who died, Frankie Mae?" she asked with suspicion. I wanted to tell her it was none of her damn business who died. Then I remembered she couldn't console me over something the world never knew about. I took in a deep breath. Lita heard my distress right away.

"I'd rather tell you later, Lita," I said calmly.

Then Lita surprised me. "Girl, I know what you mean. Everybody 'round here is tripping over Michael Jackson's death a couple of days ago. You go ahead take off all the time you need, Frankie Mae. You have served this company well for a whole lot of years. Just give me a ring when you're ready to talk or come back. I got your back," she promised.

Saying nothing, I simply thanked God silently for her patience and understanding and hung up the phone. I'll never forget the day she asked me if I was dating the superstar because of a rumor at work. She knew what the hell was going on with me. After Michael hid in the surveillance room for my award, Lita found a gold ring in the closet. She matched it against our inventory. She reminded me our store didn't carry rings in the million-dollar range.

"Have any idea where this ring came from?" she asked. I pursed my lips. As she had done many times before, Lita let me off the ropes. She gave me the ring, simply telling me to give it back to my man. Considering all this, it was time for me to honor the respect that Lita had given to me.

Michael had just married me in full spirit. Today, he talked to me gently about his mother, his children, and the world, saying he would miss everybody, but especially me. I thanked him for coming back for the wedding. Then he asked me not to cry. He said the kids were going to need me to be strong.

"Do it for them, Frankie Mae," he advised. Then he gave me seven months to get ready. He said by December 2009 we'd finally go on our honeymoon into a lifelong journey together. That was the very last moment I ever felt his touch or vividly heard his voice, for I, too, had to now mourn my man, Michael Jackson. Simply put, I had to let him go.

Today, after my shock of losing the King of Pop, I know that Michael is safe in the bosom of the Lord. Other than that, he will always be safe with me. Before you really think I'm some whack job who didn't know a hoot about Michael Jackson, you had better think again and stay with me on this. When you love a man as much as I love Michael, death can be a surreal thing to go through. I am not going to take my life; I am going to live my life in memory of Michael Jackson. I am not worried, for he knows that I will be with him one day as I promised.

The End of a Beautiful Life

His talent was legendary. Our love was the realest thing that ever happened in my life. Michael Jackson's spirit thrives within my heart. I know that I will be with him soon one day. As his mother has ordered his remains to be taken to a private place, my heart goes out to the entire Jackson family. I have read about the body being in a family crypt at Hollywood's Forest Lawn Cemetery. When I read these things I wished that December would get closer so I could finally be with my love.

As I close this chapter in my life on my special love, I am reminded that people are still moving my man's corpse to cold rooms in dark basements and it makes me scared. I have read that his beautiful mother has visited her son many times at Forest Lawn, crying and apologizing. She has nothing to apologize for. She and Joe were the best parents an aspiring artist could have. I don't know anyone who would not have appreciated the opportunities that Joe and Katherine afforded their family. Here it is now just two days after Michael's body was laid to rest on September 3, 2009. Still there have been no signs of Diana Ross.

CNN showed a little of the feed at the funeral. Again, Michael's mother was beside herself with grief. Sitting just rows behind her, I wanted to comfort Katherine, but she would not have known me from Adam. I was able to hug each of Michael's children. I got the impression from the looks in their eyes that they knew me. To me he has already reached the apex for his soul. I know I will soon be joining him there. Like Katherine, it's hard for me to let Michael go. I get peace, though, knowing that there will be no more accusations, no more trials, and most important of all, peace for Michael Jackson. For us there is no more hiding and no more cameras wanting to report an affair that was one of Michael Jackson's best-kept secrets.

As for Dr. Murray, I never trusted him when Michael first told me about him. If there were drugs, society is to blame. False accusations and multi-million-dollar companies that couldn't control a simple commercial literally formed the means to change a gentle man's life forever. So many people wanted a piece of Michael Jackson. For all the years I loved him I was true to his heart, just as I promised him I would be. I never betrayed his love in life, and I will not do it in death. The important thing for everybody to remember now is that it's over. Michael finally has the peace he wanted and needed and deserved so much.

Michael was the love of my life. I cry each time I think of him. Today, I still work at the same place I did when I met him. I am looking now into the surveillance room. I still can't believe he tucked his body in that hideaway all those years ago to watch me get an award. Today nobody will know the truth about our love until this book comes out. Michael told me to write this book the very day we started going together on that freeway. I promised him that upon his death I would tell the truth and do it within one year. And now I have. Lita will laugh her head off upon verifying her old intuition. Then she will mourn the death of my true life relationship with the world's most famous star.

THE LOVE HE SAVED

Places to Go to Remember Michael Jackson

http://articles.latimes.com/2009/jun/26/local/me-jackson-timeline26?pg=1

Some of Michael Jackson's Favored Charities

http://www.allmichaeljackson.com/charities.html

- AIDS Project L.A.
- American Cancer Society
- Angel Food
- Big Brothers of Greater LA
- BMI Foundation, Inc.
- Brotherhood Crusade
- Brothman Burn Center
- Camp Ronald McDonald
- Child help U.S.A.
- Children's Institute International
- Cities/Schools Scholarship Fund
- Elizabeth Taylor Aids Foundation
- Juvenile Diabetes Foundation
- Love Match
- Make-A-Wish Foundation
- Minority Aids Project
- Motown Museum
- NAACP
- National Rainbow Coalition
- Rotary Club of Australia
- Society of Singers
- Starlight Foundation
- The Carter Center's Atlanta Project

- The Sickle Cell Research Foundation
- Transafrica
- United Negro College Fund (UNCF)
- United Negro College Fund Ladders

Michael Jackson Albums (as an adult artist)

http://www.allmichaeljackson.com/albums.html

- Invincible
- Blood On The Dance Floor
- HIStory
- Dangerous
- Bad
- Thriller
- Off The Wall

Michael Jackson's US Number Ones

http://en.wikipedia.org/wiki/Records_and_achievements_of_Michael_Jackson

- 1972: "Ben" (1 week)
- 1979: "Don't Stop 'Til You Get Enough" (1 week)
- 1980: "Rock with You" (4 weeks)
- 1983: "Billie Jean" (7 weeks)
- 1983: "Beat It" (3 weeks)
- 1983: "Say Say Say" (6 weeks)
- 1987: "I Just Can't Stop Loving You" (with Siedah Garrett) (1 week)
- 1987: "Bad" (2 weeks)
- 1987: "The Way You Make Me Feel" (1 week)
  1988: "Man in the Mirror" (2 weeks)
- 1988: "Dirty Diana" (1 week)
- 1991: "Black or White" (7 weeks)
- 1995: "You Are Not Alone" (1 week)

Positive Ways to Honor the Memory of Michael Jackson

http://www.ehow.com/how_5123848_honor-michael-jackson.html

If you love Michael the way so many people in the world do, you can honor his life by doing some positive things to remember him by. I encourage others to support Michael's charities. Buy the albums again that you have not heard in a while. They are just as good today as they were when Michael was alive. Here are more things you can do to honor Michael Joseph Jackson's life.

Start a website for Michael Jackson fans to mourn. Allow them to post comments and mourn the famous pop star.

1. Name your child after him. This is the ultimate way to honor Michael Jackson.

2. Make a bumper sticker or car decal dedicated to Michael Jackson's memory. It could say *RIP Michael* with his birth date and date he died. You can also put this in your home.

3. Contribute to Michael Jackson's charities. You can find a list at http://www.allmichaeljackson.com/charities.html

4. Write a song or poem about Michael Jackson

and how he touched your life. Post your song/poem on various websites that mourn him.

5. Attend memorial events for Michael Jackson. There will be many for years to come.

6. Pass on his legacy to your children and grand-children. Tell them about Michael Jackson and let them hear his songs. Make them fans.

7. Michael Jackson's Family Tree

   http://www.mtv.com/news/articles/1614845/20090626/jackson_michael.jhtml

Katherine Esther Jackson (born May 4, 1930) is the matriarch of the Jackson musical family.

Joseph Walter "Joe" Jackson (born July 26, 1929) in Fountain Hill, Arkansas

http://en.wikipedia.org/wiki/Joseph_Jackson_(manager)

Michael Jackson's Father

Joseph Jackson was born in Arkansas, the eldest of four to Samuel Jackson and Crystal Lee King. His parents separated when he was twelve. He moved with his father to Oakland, California, where he lived until after turning eighteen when he moved to East Chicago, Indiana, to live near his mother. While there, he met his future wife Katherine Scruse. After a brief marriage to another woman and then an annulment, Joseph and Katherine began a courtship resulting in their November 5, 1949, wedding. Settling in Gary, Indiana, Joseph, a former boxer, worked full-time as a crane operator at Gary's U.S. Steel company, while Katherine tended to their children. In the mid-1950s, Joseph started a music career with his brother Luther, playing guitar in a band called The Falcons. The group split up a couple of years later after failing to get a recording deal. Joseph returned full-time to his job at U.S. Steel.

Michael Jackson's Siblings

Rebbie (May 29, 1950)

The oldest of the nine Jackson siblings, Rebbie didn't get a shot at stardom with her brothers. It wasn't until 1976 that she began a professional singing career, albeit one in the background: She was a backup vocalist on albums by the Emotions and other R&B acts. In 1984, fresh off the record-breaking success of *Thriller,* Michael produced Rebbie's hit single "Centipede," which rose to #4 on the R&B chart. Since then, she's come out with several albums, the last – 1998's *Yours*

Faithfully – on Michael's MJJ record label.

Jackie (May 4, 1951)

Along with Michael, he was lead singer of the Jackson 5. After recording thirteen albums for Motown, the group signed with CBS Records in 1976 and became the Jacksons. Their first few efforts faltered, but the 1978 album *Destiny* reestablished their reputation and produced a top-ten single in 1979, "Shake Your Body (Down to the Ground)." As a solo artist, Jackie released a self-titled debut in 1973 and "Be the One" in 1989.

Tito (October 15, 1953)

After the success of *Destiny*, Tito and the Jacksons released the platinum-selling *Triumph* in 1980 and the multiplatinum-selling *Victory* in 1984. After Michael and then Marlon left the band, Tito became a successful studio musician. In 1989, the Jacksons returned for a largely Michael-free album called *2300 Jackson Street,* the final Jacksons album.

Jermaine (December 11, 1954)

In 1972, while continuing to perform with his brothers, Jermaine released his first solo record, which produced the top-ten single "Daddy's Home." When the Jacksons left Motown, Jermaine left the band, as he was married to Motown founder Berry Gordy's daughter. Subsequently, he carried on releasing solo material, including hit singles like the Stevie Wonder-produced "Tell Me I'm Not Dreaming" and the dance track "Dynamite."

LaToya (May 29, 1956)

LaToya got her start singing backup vocals for the Jackson 5 and went solo with a 1980 self-titled album. She continued to churn out solo music but is perhaps best known for posing nude for *Playboy* in 1989 and writing a tell-all autobiography that led to estrangement from some of the siblings.

Marlon (March 12, 1957)

The guitarist for the family group, Marlon left in 1987 to pursue a solo career. His first single "Don't Go" – from debut album *Baby Tonight* – climbed as high as #2 on the Hot R&B chart. But Marlon's subsequent efforts proved considerably less successful. He appeared on only one track on *2300*.

Michael (August 29, 1958)

He's the King of Pop for a reason: More than 750 million records sold worldwide, eight platinum or multiplatinum albums, thirteen #1 singles, and thirteen Grammy Awards.

Randy (October 29, 1961)

Randy joined the group after Jermaine left in 1976, though he'd been performing with his brothers as a percussionist for some time. He performed on hit Jacksons albums like *Triumph* and *Victory*. Following the band's dissolution, Randy became a successful studio musician and also formed his own band, Randy & the Gypsies, which put out an album in 1989. He reunited with his brothers for *2300*.

Janet (May 16, 1966)

The youngest Jackson appeared with her siblings

onstage and on television but embarked on a solo career, starting with a 1982 self-titled record. In 1986, *Control* proved to be her breakout album, eventually going platinum five times and spawning hit singles like "When I Think of You." Her next two discs, 1989's *Janet Jackson' s Rhythm Nation 1814* and 1993's *Janet,* became even more successful, each going platinum six times.

Friday, August 28, 2009

http://omg.yahoo.com/news/coroner-jackson-death-homicide-sleep-aids-caused/27038?nc

LOS ANGELES – Right in time for what would have been Michael's 51st birthday today, Michael Jackson's death was ruled a homicide caused primarily by the powerful anesthetic Propofol and another sedative. As tears fill my eyes, I am reminded of the day I told Michael I didn't trust Dr. Murray. I didn't know the man. All I knew was that whenever he was around, Michael was not available to take personal calls. Not even his cook was allowed up in his quarters. Another cook said he saw Dr. Murray toting silver and green oxygen tanks in and out of the house. All of this was of great concern to me.

Today, the coroner made this announcement as I am putting the finishing touches on my book, *The Love He Saved.*

This ruling had been highly anticipated for a while now, as AP had already said the week before that a reliable source leaked details of the long-awaited report. The media said the ruling increases the chances of criminal charges against Michael's former personal doctor, Conrad Murray.

The coroner's office said the cause of Michael's death was "acute Propofol intoxication." It is said that other sedatives contributed to the death, including Lorazepam prescribed under the brand name Ativan.

Other drugs found in Jackson's system were: Midazolam, Diazepam, Lidocaine, and Ephedrine.

As most of the report told the true story, the coroner didn't release the full autopsy report, pending an ongoing security hold, reportedly at the request of Los Angeles authorities as they continue investigating the case.

In Closing

In time, friends and loved ones, including the kids that Michael Jackson grew to love, have convinced me that my beloved Michael Jackson is in a better place. For days all I could do was cry and cry over Michael. Each tribute hurt. Each reminder of his leaving makes me want to die and be with him. Writing this book was a therapy that Michael's spirit gave to me. He gave me the courage and the spirit to tell my love story.

Now you know what a magnificent life I had with Michael Jackson that started when I was a mere sixteen years old. Believe in yourself and love the ones who love you.

Rest in Peace, Michael Jackson. The world loves you!

Michael Jackson Official Website
http://www.michaeljackson.com/

http://www.mjfanclub.net/home/index.php

Ultimate Fan-Based Michael Jackson Links

MOONWALKER

http://www.geocities.com/hampton0531/MOONWALKER.html

I just started, so there's not much Michael Jackson moonwalker.

MJJMoa Remixes

http://www.mjjmoa.com

This site brings to you all of my own remixes.

King Of Pop - Hungarian Michael Jackson Fan Site

http://www.kingofpop.hu/

The Michael Jackson Source Forum

http://www.mjjsource.proboards53.com

The Michael Jackson Source is one of the hottest all-new fan forums on the net! Opened just days ago, join now to become one of the first members of this exciting new club!

Michael Jackson Online Auction

http://mjsite.shopcheap.com

Buy & sell Michael Jackson memorabilia! Free to list! List as many as you want.

Michael Jackson & The Jackson 5

http://www.mjsite.com

This is a Michael Jackson fan website. We have many pictures (rare), a Michael Jackson auction, forum, stories, etc.

Michael Jackson Trader

http://www.michael-jackson-trader.com

A Michael Jackson music and memorabilia store. A range of CDs, vinyl, clothing, and many other collectibles.

All Michael Jackson

http://www.allmichaeljackson.com

Full of information on all aspects of Michael's career as an adult artist. Kept up to date with latest news and photos.

Michael Jackson The King Of Pop

http://www.mjtkop.com

Fan site with the latest news and information on the King of Pop, huge gallery, interactive features, articles, forums, and more.

Come Together for Michael

http://www.freewebs.com/cometogetherformicheal

A Michael Jackson site with updated news and photos. Also has a guestbook, poems, and artwork.

Innocent Michael

http://www.freewebs.com/innocentmichael

My cool Michael Jackson site with news, pictures, wallpapers, events, poems, etc.

Unbreakable Michael Jackson

http://s13.invisionfree.com/UnbreakableMJ

Michael Jackson forum and latest news.

MJIFC: Michael Jackson Internet Fan Club

http://www.mjifc.nl

Michael Jackson Internet Fanclub. The #1 source for fans. Features the latest news, pictures, downloads, lyrics, famous quotes, forum, chatbox and much, much more!

Michael Jackson - BlackFedora.Net

http://www.blackfedora.net

MICHAEL JACKSON data bank

http://www.mjdatabank.com

French fan site about the King of Pop. All aspects of his career vividly described with extensive discography and always updated news section.

Michael Jackson Remixed

http://mjremixed.tricky3.co.uk

A website dedicated to remixes of Michael Jackson's songs. Includes a full, comprehensive database of remixes (official, promo, and bootleg).

MJNewsOnline

http://www.mjnewsonline.com

Michael Jackson website featuring chat, discussion, and the latest news.

Official Site

http://www.mjnet.com

Michael Jackson Music Links

Michael Jackson Official Web Site
http://www.michaeljackson.com

Michael Jackson official site at Sony Music allows users to research the King of Pop by reading his career history, viewing his complete discography with song samples, viewing photos, and watching short films. Visit the MJ Interactive section for AIM buddy icons and wallpaper. Website has a link to the Sony Music Store.

Michael Jackson Trader
http://www.michael-jackson-trader.com

One of the largest resources for MJ memorabilia and collectibles on the Net, this site sells and trades singles, CDs, cassettes, autographs, books and magazines, videos and DVDs, apparel, stickers, dolls, and much more. Items are conveniently organized in a catalogue index. Find ordering instructions, newsletter subscriptions, and club memberships.

All Michael Jackson
http://www.allmichaeljackson.com

Michael Jackson extensive fan site offers monthly news updates, a biography, a filmography, bibliography of books written about the pop legend, a photo gallery, a list of his rarely-given interviews, and instructions on how to mimic his most famous dance move, the moonwalk. Music section includes album reviews, a list of achievements, lyrics, videographer, and a tour chronology. The MJ Store features links where albums and other merchandise can be purchased.

Michael Jackson at the Sony Music Store
http://shop.myplay.com/search.htm?keyword=michael+jackson

Purchase the pop artist's entire discography direct from his record label. Includes album reviews, release dates, and track listings for every album.

Michael Jackson Fan Club
http://www.mjfanclub.net/

Endorsed by the music legend himself, this fan club offers weekly news updates, includes links to his biography, key facts, videographer, descriptions of books he's written, a list of awards, and a photo gallery.

Michael Jackson CDs at Amazon.com
Shop for every album in the King of Pop's discography, including singles, imports, special editions, and karaoke CDs. Read album reviews, see customer ratings, and listen to song samples.

M-Jackson.com - The Path To The Future
http://www.m-jackson.com/

Michael Jackson supporters provide frequent news updates in regards to his court cases and CD releases, a shop with items such as glitter gloves, information about his charity, "Heal The World," and his career history. Enter the forum to interact with other fans.

Michael Jackson Books: Amazon.com
Browse a selection of official and unauthorized biographies, anthologies, and books written by the star himself. Autobiographies and essay collections include *Moonwalk* and *Dancing the Dream: Poems and Reflections*

Michael Jackson: AMG
http://www.allmusic.com/cg/amg.dll?p=amg&sql=11:5q4tk5ax9kr0

Profile of the singer includes a biography, a full discography with song samples, and a list of similar artists and musical followers. Become a registered member to see a complete song list, credits, and list of awards.

Michael Jackson Music at EBay

This online auction's stock of The Gloved One's music is constantly turning over, and includes singles, CDs, LPs, singles, imports, posters, promos, and rare releases. See photos and descriptions of each item before bidding.

MTV.com

Artist profile features a nice selection of audio/video clips, a biography, dozens of news headlines, ringtones available for purchase, a discography with links to purchase the albums, and photo flipbooks.

Michael Jackson Entertainment Memorabilia: EBay

Features items related to Jackson's entire career, with collector's items related to music, movies, and television. Items for sale include posters, buttons, stickers, lighters, tour jackets, books, magazines, autographs, clippings, and costumes.

Michael Jackson: AZLyrics

Boasts a complete collection of lyrics, listed by album. Click on a song title to see full lyrics.

Michael Jackson DVDs & Movies: EBay

Find recordings of Jackson's numerous appearances on film and television, including taped interviews, rare performances, concerts, making-of videos, documentaries, and films he's appeared in such as *The Wiz*. Offers selections on DVD, VHS, and laserdisc, both new and used.

<u>The HIStory of Michael Jackson's Face</u>
http://www.anomalies-unlimited.com/Jackson.html

Provides a photographic history with witty commentary about the numerous changes Jackson's face has undergone due to repeated cosmetic surgeries. See photos of his face pre-surgery, starting in 1979, with changes throughout the years up to the present. Commentary includes notes on what was happening in his life and career at the time of the rumored surgery.

<u>Michael Jackson For Sale</u>
http://www.michaeljacksonforsale.com

The ultimate collectors' website. Unusual offerings like the albums on vinyl, vintage tour programs, and original Jackson Five memorabilia. Shop is based in the UK but ships worldwide.

<u>Michael Jackson on Wikipedia</u>
http://en.wikipedia.org/wiki/Michael_Jackson

An extensive MJ bio, with separate articles covering the 1993 allegations of child molestation, his marriages and children, and his 2005 trial.

<u>Yahoo! Shopping</u>
Shopping collection features over 25 pages of Michael Jackson collectibles and merchandise for sale, with prices and item descriptions. Items include autographs, CDs, LPs, DVDs, books, 12-inch mixes, and apparel.

Michael Jackson World Network
http://www.mjworld.net
A global fan site featuring news, a newsletter, articles and photos. Unusual memorabilia for sale, including the *Santa Maria Times* newspaper from the day he was found not guilty of charges of child molestation.

Michael Jackson Posters: AllPosters.com
Carries a wide selection of framed and unframed posters and prints, including promotional posters and concert posters. See size dimensions and prices.

Resources

CNN

Wordup Magazine

Newsweek Magazine

Wikipedia

Carol Denise Mitchell

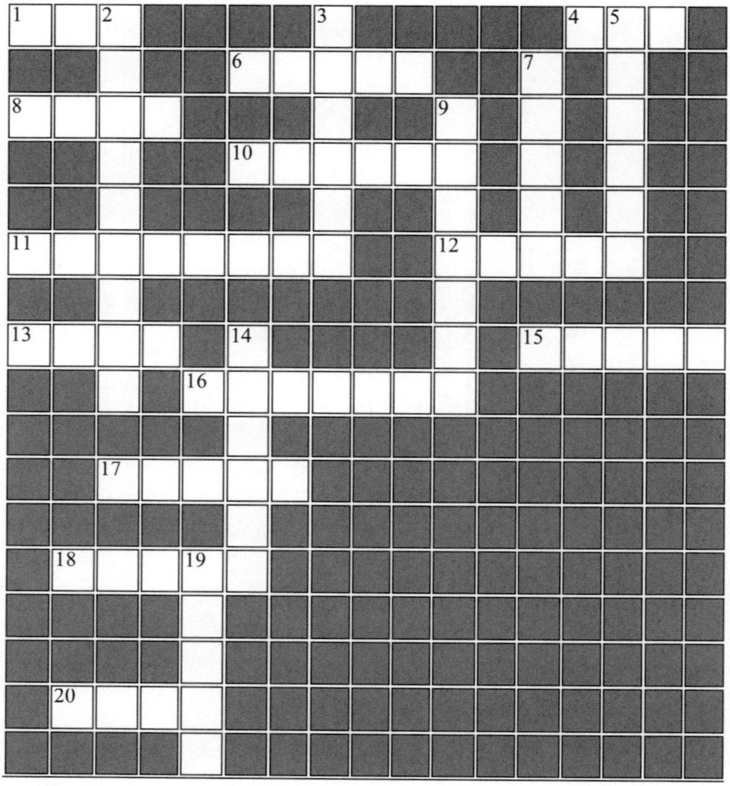

THE LOVE HE SAVED

Copy these crossword puzzles for your friends. See how good they are at solving the puzzles!

ACROSS

1. Wesley Snipes
4. The Wall
6. 2005
8. Jackie
10. Katherine
11. Michael Jackson
13. 1993
15. June
16. Jermaine
17. Elizabeth
18. Culkin
20. Elvis

DOWN

2. Remember the times
3. Janet
5. Joe
7. Cover
9. Jermaine
14. Brooke
19. Lisa

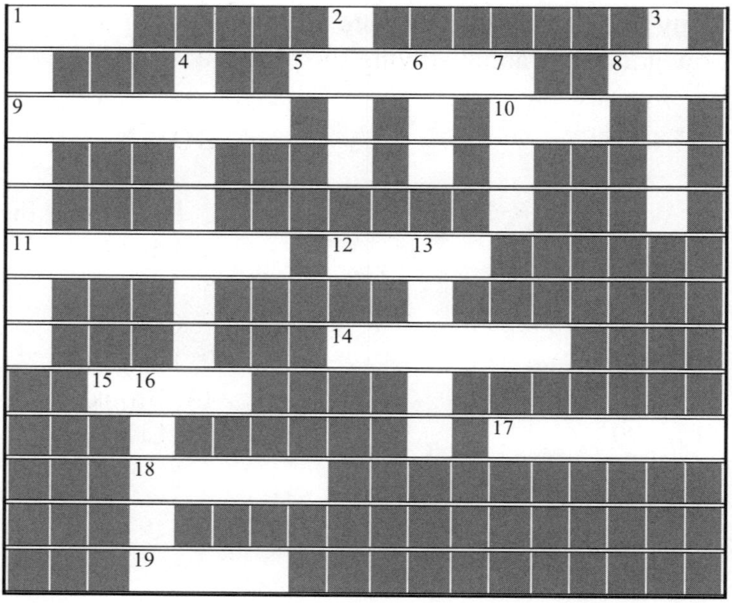
1
2
3
4
5
6
7
8
9
10
11
12
13
14
15
16
17
18
19

THE LOVE HE SAVED

ACROSS

1. Ben
5. Latoya
8. Prince
9. Jackson
10. The Wall
11. Tito
12. The Love
14. Carey
15. Indiana
17. Jean
18. Gordy
19. One

DOWN

1. The Time
2. Of Pop
3. Ross
4. Paris
6. Wiz
7. With you
13. Winfrey
16. Thriller

Michael Jackson Stores
http://michaeljackson.shop.bravadousa.com/

Trade Memorabilia
http://www.michael-jackson-trader.com/

Michael Jackson Online Stores
http://eil.com/artist/michael-jackson.asp

Michael Jackson Official Merchandise
http://michaeljacksonmerch.sparkart.net/

Michael Jackson is Dead
http://www.merch.com/MICHAEL-JACKSON/products/948/

Michael Jackson Childhood Photos
http://www.hotklix.com/content/entertainment/celebs/Michael-jackson-rare-childhood-photos

Michael Jackson Poetry
http://www.scribd.com/doc/17245289/Michael-Jackson-Poetry-For-The-King

http://www.mjquotes.com/poetry.htm

http://hubpages.com/hub/afewpoemsformichaeljackson

Michael Jackson Letters

http://charityathomas.blogspot.com/2005/11/open-letter-to-michael-jackson.html

Michael Jackson's Favorite Song, Smile:

http://www.nowpublic.com/culture/michael-jacksons-favorite-song-smile-charlie-chaplin

Lyrics:

Smile though your heart is aching
Smile even though its breaking
When there are clouds in the sky, you'll get by
If you smile with your fear and sorrow
Smile and maybe tomorrow
You'll find that life is still worthwhile

If you just
Light up your face with gladness
Hide every trace of sadness
Although a tear may be ever so near
That's the time you must keep on trying
Smile, what's the use of crying?
You'll find that life is still worthwhile

If you just
Smile though your heart is aching
Smile even though its breaking
When there are clouds in the sky, you'll get by
If you smile through your fear and sorrow
Smile and maybe tomorrow

You'll find that life is still worthwhile
If you just smile

that's the time you must keep on trying
Smile, what's the use of crying?
You'll find that life is still worthwhile
If you just smile

Order Form ©Carol Mitchell Books

Name: [redacted]

Address:

Mail Orders to: Post Office Box 484, Concord, California 94522-

Home Phone: Or Call: 925-435-8699

Select any one of or *more* than one of the following books for order:

- The Love He Saved – Price per unit/book=$19.95
- Rovella Starr (*A Love Starved Bitch*) - Price per unit/book=$19.95
- Your Rights, (*Employment Rights handbook*) Price per unit/book=$21.95

- Michael Jackson T-Shirt (*with the book cover*) Price per unit/book=$20.00
- Michael Jackson Hat (*with the book cover*) Price per unit/book=$20.00

Thank you for sending my order to:

Your Name:		
Your Street Address:		**Apt. #:**
City:	**State:**	**Zip Code:**

[redacted]

CDM has a **NO REFUND POLICY** on all books unless it is an overpayment, duplicate payment, or program is cancelled by CMB. It is our policy to produce state-of-the art books. If you have any questions please feel free to write CMB @ acceptedletter@gmail.com or write to us at CMB Post Office Box 484 Concord California 94522-0484.